BROKEN

THE BREACH CHRONICLES BOOK ONE

IVY LOGAN

Edited by
DUCKMAN PROOFREADING

THE BREACH CHRONICLES BOOK I

Broken But Not Lost

BROKEN

A Gripping Young Adult Romance & Supernatural Fantasy
Adventure

Broken: The Breach Chronicles Book I
Copyright © 2017 Ivy Logan
Published by Broken
ISBN:978-93-5288-595-4

Book Cover Art and Titles © Ivy Logan- Created by Mario Teodesio

Website, Character Design and Book Cover © Ivy Logan by Ideascope Team

Character designs by Marcus Corraya & Pearl Fernandes.

Overall Look by Vishvesh Desai.

Editing, Proofreading, and Formatting by Abbie Lee of Duckman Proofreading

PROLOGUE

*E*vil has many faces. Vanquish it at its genesis before it spreads its vicious tentacles is what the wise would advise. But sometimes evil is disguised in a cloak of innocence and its true nature remains hidden.

Damien's fascination with violence probably began a long time ago when he was just a boy of six who had a rendezvous with death and survived. But no one would be able to pinpoint the exact moment when his tryst with evil began.

It was a time of war between humans and their sworn adversaries, the supernaturals. Amidst an atmosphere of distrust and hate began the *Purge*, the great war between humans and supernaturals, with each side trying to annihilate the other.

Damien had never seen giants or werewolves before, and even as his human family succumbed to the brutality of the conflict, the little boy had eyes only for the giants, majestic but vicious and half blind. Just the heel of a giant could smash the little one to bits, but did he notice? No. The colossal creatures captivated the boy so much that they drove him to flaunt an utter and complete disregard for his own life as he stood dumbstruck staring up at them.

This was probably the only time he displayed such foolhardy behaviour, because the man Damien would grow up to become would never risk his life in such a fashion for any reason whatsoever.

THE HEICHI WERE a clan of sorceresses, the most powerful among all supernaturals. Ava was one of their Elders, a firstborn among the immortal sorceresses. Each of them had a gift, a special power. Ava's was her sight. Ava had no mastery over her visions, and if an event in the future was sufficiently potent and forceful, it drew her to it across the lines of time. This abrupt travel through space and time often ravaged her until she realized it was better to accept the pull than to fight it.

Ava usually took the advice of her best friend and protector, Siobhan. Siobhan was an Elder like her, but she was also the queen of the Heichi. Her exquisite beauty was legendary, as was her knowledge, ageless and flavoured with wisdom and experience that only an immortal destined to be a queen could enjoy. Ava literally had to look up to the much taller Siobhan, who always wore elegance effortlessly in a finely flowing sheath wrapped around her like a cocoon and shimmering like a waterfall. The beauty of the Heichi sorceresses was so glorious that it had a tendency to turn humans into gibbering fools; it therefore was usually toned down. But as Siobhan generally stayed away from mankind and their ilk, she let her beauty shine through, unvarnished and unimpeded.

Ava's focus remained on blending in with humans by playing down her ethereal beauty and garbing herself in wools, capes and tunics. Having to disguise her voluminous, soft curls as blue as the colour of the day sky that would otherwise be cascading over her delicate shoulders almost to her knees was a difficult task for Ava. Blue hair was not a colour a human would ignore. The secret of the Heichi legacy lay in the cerulean blue of their hair. Even the strongest of spells would never be able to alter its colour. Chop it off and the magic would be lost.

THE PURGE WAS such a great event that it pulled Ava from the past. Seeing the little boy about to be smashed to smithereens, she snatched him away right from under the colossal foot of a giant. Her soft-hearted nature saved Damien's life. In her own time, the other sorceresses called her Ava the Merciful, because she could never see another in pain or danger.

As Damien stared transfixed at the face of the cloaked woman with slender brows, soothing hazel eyes and an unblemished face that shone with a mystical grace, Ava was unmindful of his adoring gaze. In her haste to save the child, she had disobeyed Siobhan. It would have taken a heartless person to stand back and watch a cherubic child trampled to death. Ava did not have a mean bone in her body, so she had rushed to the rescue. She had saved the boy, but in doing so, she meddled with time. She had gone against Siobhan, who had expressly forbidden her from intervening in events of the future.

If only Ava could leave Damien behind. But to whom would she entrust this little boy? His family was dead. Almost everyone else was dead too. She saw no women around, at least none who were living—the dead were far too many.

The men who still lived were violent, intent on killing and attacking supernaturals, including her. How could she leave this defenceless child with bloodthirsty killers even if they were human?

In the past, which is where Ava came from, the eagle eyes of Siobhan awaited her. If Ava took Damien back, her best friend would be both appalled and terrified of the consequences of Ava's utter disregard for orders.

The other sorceresses, eager to cause discord between the two Elder sorceresses, would interpret Ava's disobedience as an act of mutiny rather than humanity. They would use it as fodder to drive a wedge between Siobhan and Ava. No, she couldn't take Damien to the past, but he wasn't safe in his own time. So that only left the future.

Ava took the boy many years ahead of his own time. She loved children, and furthermore, she felt responsible for the fate of this little one she had saved. Having watched his family and his people mowed down by giants or cut to pieces by werewolves and other creatures was more than enough of a cross for a child to bear in one lifetime. Those pure of heart and mind often tend to see others in the same halo of goodness. Ava only saw the innocence; she saw none of the guile or speculation in Damien's eyes.

Ava belatedly realized that the time she chose to take Damien to seemed to be devoid of supernaturals, but she didn't have the time to look for them. She had to return to the past, otherwise Siobhan would suspect something had gone wrong. The humans barely remembered the existence of sorceresses and other supernatural folk. She hoped that this new environment would work in Damien's favour and give him a fresh start. She wanted the child to forget the torment he had been through. She hoped he would find nothing but happiness with his new family.

Ava noticed Damien's lack of tears. She assumed the boy failed to grieve for his family because he was in shock. How could she know that even as a child, Damien was already shrewd, manipulative and thinking one step ahead?

Ava left Damien in the custody of the childless king and queen of Aberevon. She believed this way the boy would be loved, would be safe, and would want for nothing.

The queen welcomed Ava's gift with all her heart, but the king looked upon Ava with suspicion. He hated this young child that the stranger had thrust upon him, but he did not want to disappoint his queen, so he smiled his acquiescence. The boy looked like a weakling; the king hoped he would not survive past his tenth year. His queen could enjoy the bliss of motherhood for a while, but hopefully he would not have to crown an outsider as his heir. The king did not know he would not live to see how wrong he was.

Before Ava left, Damien caught her hand. "Thank you for saving me," he said, his voice suffused with gratitude.

Overcome by maternal feelings, Ava made another mistake. "You are very welcome, Damien," she replied. "This is what we do." She unwittingly told him more than she should have.

"We?" he asked.

Charmed by the innocence of the child, she answered, "Me and my sisters. Others just like me."

"What if something happens here? Will you come back for me, or send your sisters to get me? What if you die too, like my parents? Who will look after me? This king and queen, or your sisters?" he asked bitterly, somehow feeling apprehensive about his new home.

"Only happiness awaits you in Aberevon. I have looked into your new mother. She is the epitome of kindness. I would never hand you over to a stranger just like that. As for me, I cannot return here, but you will always find me somewhere on Earth because I must already exist somewhere in this timeline." She fell silent. Ava realized that in her haste to reassure the child, she had again told him too much.

Damien's eyes sparkled with understanding. "Are you one of them?" he asked. "One of the immortal sorceresses?"

Ava gasped. Damien's astuteness took her by surprise. How could he be aware of the existence of the Heichi sorceresses at only six? She did not know too much about children. Were they usually this aware? Maybe they picked up more than they should. It didn't matter, as she intended to wipe Damien's memories clean of the past, otherwise it would be too dangerous for him and for other magical beings, who seemed to have hidden themselves. The

Purge must have permanently destroyed the already tense relations between the two factions, but the disappearance of the supernaturals from the future would have to remain a secret from the other Heichi for now.

Ava faced another hurdle. Little Damien had his own secrets. The biggest one was, of course, his resistance to her memory-wiping spell. For some reason, Ava's magic was ineffectual on him. He remembered everything but chose to keep this from Ava. When she asked him if he knew who she was, he feigned a blank look. She looked deep into his eyes and saw no recognition in the slightest. Ava left, secure in the belief that Damien was now free of the past, although this was a falsehood perpetrated by Damien for reasons best known to him.

Existing in one time and retaining echoes of a past life and world would always ensure Damien's memories were torn between the life he remembered and the life he was living. He would eventually be a man who inspired fear and hate with no hope for redemption.

Ava wouldn't learn the truth until it was too late. Her actions would irrevocably impact the future and she would only get one opportunity to right a grave wrong.

CHAPTER I

I never knew being suspended in time could be such torture.
It is not easy waiting on the outside when every fibre of my being is
crying for the impossible, a simple touch, a smile or a word from a loved
one. I presumed I knew pain, but being invisible to the ones I love hurts
like nothing has ever hurt before. My soul yearns for them.
I can only console myself with the certainty that this was my preor-
dained destiny because it all started long before me with my mother,
Caitlin.
Talia

~

THE BIRTH OF A SORCERESS—CAITLIN
Three years after the Purge, the great war between the
humans and supernaturals...

THE WATER of the Well of Creation foamed and bubbled. A
sorceress was coming. To Siobhan's relief, the well's surface was

layered with white flowers—*white*—a symbol of the coming of a guardian sorceress.

Every sorceress in the Heichi clan had a purpose and a role to play. The magical powers of the well denoted their roles through the colours of the flowers that bloomed before the birth of a sorceress. This was the first time white flowers had bloomed because this was the very first guardian ordained by the Well of Creation.

Ava volunteered to be the first of the *guardians*, the only Heichi sorceresses who still lived on Earth, and because of her, other sorceresses followed suit. The mutual hate and suspicion between humans and the supernaturals led to a war with many innocents dying on both sides.

Most of the supernaturals left their earthly abode soon after the war ended and formed their own magical realm parallel to Earth—Htrae. But old habits die hard, and every so often, one of the supernaturals would stray back to Earth. Earth was once their home after all, so it was only natural they were still drawn to it. Ava and the other guardians always stood between them and the humans.

The humans had long forgotten about the existence of super-naturals—with good reason. Some of the supernatural clans had enjoyed hunting humans for mere sport.

Siobhan didn't abide by the idea of leaving humans at the mercy of violent and aggressive supernaturals. Neither did she want the humans to declare another war against them, hence the sisterhood of the guardians was very important to her. The guardians always found the stray fugitives and sent them back to Htrae. If a human saw a supernatural, the guardians would wipe their memory clean. It was now three years after the Purge, and this was the very first guardian sorceress that the Well of Creation was sending them. The guardians had been spread thin with their dual duties of protecting humans and supernaturals from each other, so Siobhan was very excited about this special addition.

Fortunately, the newborn was unaware of the excitement surrounding her birth. It would have confounded her beyond measure. As it were, she emerged from the hallowed waters of the Well of Creation disoriented and as wobbly as a newborn fawn.

The ancient and broken down well attracted neither humans nor thirsty animals. The Heichi left their hallowed well in a state of disrepair without any magical safeguards because they knew the nature of humans and their propensity to arrive at conclusions based on merely external appearances. Seeing the antiquated well, their eyes just slid over it because to them, it was a decrepit old structure that had been part of the scenery since who knows when. If anyone did give it a second look, it was only to infer that its waters would probably be rancid and putrid and all things terrible. The truth was, without the magical waters of the Well of Creation, the Heichi sorceresses' magic would gradually die out.

Siobhan's gentle hands supported and steadied the newborn's young body, fragile and weak from disuse. When Siobhan stumbled, Ava stepped in to lend a hand. Together they helped the young one to her feet.

When the newcomer lifted her head, both Ava and Siobhan gasped. She was the mirror image of Ava except for her eyes; while Ava's were hazel, her twin had eyes of the bluest blue, clear and beautiful like the waters of a calm lake. The newborn spotted the resemblance too.

Ava and the newborn exchanged timid smiles, a strong bond of friendship surging between them. When the rest of the sorceresses christened their new sister 'Caitlin', Ava was the first one to envelope Caitlin in a warm hug.

As Caitlin grew in awareness, she felt great power coursing through her. Her body tingled and sparked as though a fire was surging through it. As she adapted to her divinity, the elusive and ancient knowledge of the Heichi became hers and her confusion slipped further away. The anticipation of an exciting new voyage made her pulse quicken. The soft blue eyes of the young sorceress flitted from the smiling faces surrounding her to the myriad colours and shapes of her new world with unabashed curiosity.

"Welcome, child," said Siobhan lightly, for it was her responsibility to make a newborn sorceress feel contented and safe. However, as she looked at Caitlin, Siobhan sensed that this sorceress was different from all the others who had come before her but couldn't put her finger on what is was that was different. It was not just her startling resemblance to Ava; her expression was also identical to Ava's, benign and aware. It did not just shine with joy or anticipation alone. There was something more.

Ava was an Elder and an ancient sorceress, one of the most powerful in the clan. Her awareness came from a great knowledge and ancient wisdom. How could Caitlin already be a full-fledged sorceress like Ava?

Usually, when a sorceress emerged fully formed from a neverending vacuum and an ocean of emptiness, she was lost, but not Caitlin. Why? Siobhan discreetly took Ava aside, seeking her counsel. There was no better person she could talk to. "What do you think about our new sorceress?" the queen asked her friend.

"Apart from her resemblance to me?" smiled Ava. "She does seem divergent," confirmed Ava. "Caitlin is as learned and as powerful as you even though she has only just emerged from the birthing well."

"How is it possible? Ancient knowledge flows in waves. When I took my first step out of the well, you were there to help me adapt. Even though I was to be crowned queen, my powers came to me gradually over time. A newborn with all her powers at birth? How did she survive the onslaught of such tremendous power?" asked Siobhan in disbelief. "It has never happened before."

"It has. It has occurred before. Caitlin is not the first," Ava confessed. "There has been one other like her."

"Another newborn sorceress with full power from birth itself?"

asked a shocked Siobhan. "How do I not remember? Did she not survive?"

Ava smiled mysteriously. Seeing Siobhan's puzzled expression, she added softly, "It was before your time."

"How can that be when the only one who came from the well before me was you?" asked Siobhan.

"You are right." Ava smiled. "And here I am standing right in front of you."

Siobhan fell silent. She realized she had never asked Ava how it felt to be the first of their kind. She had always taken Ava's good counsel and fortitude for granted and never given any thought to her past. Siobhan felt her face flame with shame and regret.

Ava knew what Siobhan was thinking. "I handled it fine and I do okay, don't I? I am sure Caitlin will be fine too." Hoping to distract the distressed Siobhan, Ava added, "It is a pity she can't accompany you to Htrae. The new sorceresses always bloom under you."

"You already know that Caitlin is a guardian and can't leave Earth, which means you are just trying to make me feel better. But how can I forgive myself? What kind of a friend am I if I have never bothered to ask about your life?" said Siobhan.

At the mention of the reality that a guardian wasn't allowed to leave Earth on account of their obligations, Siobhan saw the brief disquiet on Ava's face, which vanished as quickly as it came. *No point in beating around the bush*, thought Siobhan. *Better to confront the matter head on*. "I know you don't always agree with the rules, Ava. You and the other guardians want to visit Htrae; it is also your home. But being decreed as a guardian means your duty to Earth comes first. The Wraith, the spirits of our revered ancestors, have their reasons for putting such ancient canons and decrees in place, otherwise there would be chaos on Earth."

"So how will Caitlin cope without your help?" asked a worried Ava. She was eager to change the topic. Their debate on the lack

11

of permission for the guardians to enter Htrae was a huge thorn in her side. She would rather not talk about it anymore.

"I know of a guardian sorceress who always sees the best in everyone around her. She has faith in the goodness of others. Her strength and serenity are an inspiration to many, including me. I would like her to be Caitlin's mentor," said Siobhan.

"Wonderful idea!" exclaimed Ava. "Come, let us talk to Caitlin's mentor together. Who is it? Wait, let me guess; is it Angela, or is it Krysta, or maybe Ruth?"

"Ava, I am talking about *you*," said Siobhan. "If Caitlin's powers get out of control, they could turn inwards and turn her light into darkness. She really needs your help. You are the only one who has already established a bond with her. The others you speak of are wise too, but they don't have the same connection with Caitlin as you seem to. I know I already ask so much of you, but do you see yourself finding time for her?"

"Flattery will get you everywhere," Ava commented dryly. "You are aware that as queen, you could have just commanded instead of requesting." Ava admonished Siobhan gently. "You have got to stop being such a democratic leader. Some of the sorceresses already take advantage of your inclusive nature to further their own agendas."

"But not you," said Siobhan. "And that is why I will always depend on you. It is not in your nature to misuse power, just as being an autocratic queen is not in mine," answered Siobhan without taking any offence.

"Fair enough," said Ava. "To each one her own. We did vow that we would never try to change each other but remain friends despite the differences in our nature. So, it is decided. Caitlin is now my responsibility. I will be her friend and mentor."

Siobhan's grateful smile conveyed her thanks, and the two sorceresses felt relief that the cause of their worry had been addressed.

Their words, though, had the opposite effect on Caitlin.

Having heard snippets of the exchange between Siobhan and Ava, all the gladness that warmed her heart just a while ago melted away. Her confidence and courage began to evaporate. She was different. *How? Why?* She wanted to be a part of a family, one of the many—not unique or alone.

As Caitlin tried to understand what she had heard, worry overwhelmed her and her head began to throb. Her eyes burned. She felt overwhelmed. The words flowed to Caitlin's mouth as she spoke for the first time, her voice sounding slightly gravelly and rough. "Why am I a divergent, a deviant?" She sounded like a scared young girl.

Siobhan replied in a soothing voice. "Being different is not a bad thing. You are the first of your kind and have been long awaited. You have powers that many sorceresses and guardians assembled here don't have. Why should that upset you?" The other sorceresses stood back, but Caitlin could see the under-standing on their faces, many of them offering her encouraging smiles. She began to feel better.

"How do I integrate myself with the others?" persisted Caitlin in her eagerness to blend in.

"By being yourself," said Siobhan. Seeing Caitlin's confused expression, she added, "Each of us are unique in our own way. Htrae and Earth need us for what we are, for the value each one of us brings." Seeing the recognition on Caitlin's face at the mention of Htrae, Siobhan asked in amazement, "Do you already know of our realm?"

"I don't know how but I do," answered Caitlin, nodding in affirmation, her eyes bright with worry.

"The world of humans is called Earth and the realm or sanc-tuary for supernaturals, our home, is known as Htrae. Man's enmity and hatred of supernaturals is a legacy of the past, but this past has left some open wounds, hence a few of us bear the burden of being guardians." Siobhan paused to see if Caitlin understood what she had said. The newborn was paying rapt attention.

Siobhan smiled. The child was waiting to hear more about her role in the whole scheme of things. Her face was quite easy to read. Siobhan didn't disappoint her. "Your path has already been defined. You are a guardian too, the only line of protection between humans and supernaturals. Earth is your home and your responsibility to protect. Take pride in your role."

Caitlin remained silent for a while, absorbing Siobhan's words. Siobhan sounded so profound. Caitlin looked lost in thought as a frown creased her otherwise flawless forehead. Siobhan and Ava exchanged glances, wondering if they had been too hasty in being open about her capabilities. Had they only succeeded in scaring her? Caitlin was indeed feeling slightly dazed and out of her depth. Was she as overwhelmed as she looked?

CHAPTER II

I compelled the supernatural spirits to take me with them when they came for another. I stubbornly refused to let him go and offered myself in return. The spirits agreed but it was not yet my time.
Now the unknown beckons and I am scared, for I just have to walk a few steps and the thrall of the past will no longer hold me. The glimpses I keep having of the ones I left behind will stop. The torment will end, but I cannot yet walk away because of Aiden's love and the promise I made to him—they hold me back. Will I spend eternity poised between the unknown and a life I once treasured?
Talia

THE PROPHECY—CAITLIN

AS SHE STOOD STARING at her own feet, she heard a sorceress whisper to Siobhan. "It is time. Ella is ready."

"Caitlin, I apologize. We will have to continue this conversa-

15

tion because we all have another gathering to go to. Can you join us too? It is a special one," said Siobhan, her voice taking on a secretive tone.

As Caitlin smiled in agreement, she looked up to see the sorceress gesture towards a pristine, shimmering altar she had failed to notice earlier. Everyone had already started heading towards it. All it took was one look towards the altar and Caitlin knew what it was for. This was a *gathering*, but Ella, a sister sorceress, was departing this world, not entering it like Caitlin.

Ella was a Heichi sorceress who had enjoyed an existence of almost a century before she chose to renounce her immortality and enter the Ether World, the existence beyond immortality. She had lived a long and eventful life before deciding to move on. An infinite life could become a curse, and like many of her sisters before her, rather than endure, she would shape-shift into a mortal creature of her choice, like a bird or a butterfly, and move into the afterlife beyond.

As one sister abandoned eternity, a fledgling sorceress took her place. As the ancient knowledge of the ritual flowed to her mind, Caitlin realized the importance of the gift that Ella had given her. She was to take Ella's place in this world. It was time to forget her own confusion for a while and to honour Ella as she set off on her new journey.

As the sorceresses slowly moved towards Ella, attention shifted from Caitlin, who could finally sigh in relief. She had learned one new thing about herself. She hated being the centre of attention. She enjoyed being a part of the crowd.

Siobhan and the others went on ahead. Caitlin wanted to join them in sending Ella off to the Ether World, but all thoughts flew out of her mind when she sensed someone watching her. She looked around but there was no one was in sight. She could see the others a little ahead, bonding and offering Ella their valedictions and blessings. Their proximity gave her the courage to move towards them.

Caitlin just managed to convince herself that she had only imagined the feeling of being watched and pursued when she felt something cold and invisible trail past her cheek. Her composure slowly turned to horror as whoever it was stilled at the back of her neck. She wanted to scream a warning to the others and to ask for their help but the words seemed to choke in her throat.

"Listen and listen well, Caitlin."

They knew her name. Unmindful of her terror, the voices continued tonelessly and without any emotion. The reaction they wrought from the young sorceress was anything but calm. She felt trapped and unable to escape.

A chorus of eerie and indistinct whispers pleaded with her in a painful litany. *"A warning to you we bring. Hear our voices and not your heart, for nothing but disaster it will bring. A man will come into your life when you expect not, and things will never be the same. For the sake of the child born of this union, you will your family betray. Be warned and be wise and from him stay away."*

The harsh whispers went on and on until Caitlin dropped to her knees, her head bent in surrender and defeat. *Please stop*, she cried silently. Then, as if in answer to her unspoken plea, a soft chanting with a ring of solemnity and sadness reached her ears. Amazingly, the voices in her head fell silent. Caitlin did not wait. She rose and ran towards the others, who, distracted by the ceremony, failed to notice the state she was in.

Caitlin managed to maintain the barest degree of composure as she stood at the fringe of the crowd. Ella's *Rite of Passage* was an intense sacrament with a great many sorceresses there to pay respects.

A still nervous Caitlin saw all the sorceresses bow their heads as pale, grey apparitions became visible around Ella. "The Wraith are our spirit guides. They are Heichi sisters who choose to exist in the vacuum between life and the afterlife, watching over us and assisting all immortals and supernaturals when their time comes," whispered a sorceress to Caitlin, giving her a warm smile.

Caitlin smiled back but barely heard the friendly sorceress as she couldn't get the voices out of her head. Would Ava know anything about them? Would she be able to help her? Despite being engrossed in her own thoughts, Caitlin noticed that the gathered sorceresses kept a safe distance from the Wraith. *Is it respect or fear that these spirits command?* she wondered.

As they moved deeper into the ceremony, Caitlin focused her eyes on Ella, bidding a silent farewell as she disappeared from sight in the form of a little hummingbird. The chants grew softer, signalling that the sacred ceremony was drawing to a close.

Impatient to get a better view of the spirits before they were gone, Caitlin leaned forward slightly. Later it would seem implausible to Caitlin but at that moment, it was as if her slight movement caused a shift in the air and wrecked the delicate balance between the life and the afterlife.

Caitlin watched in shock as the apparitions turned their heads in her direction. Recognition burned in their translucent eyes. As they pointed their fingers at her, an eerie but familiar scream emerged from their mouths as though the very sight of her was painful to them. Caitlin recognized them too. Her silent, hypnotic stare became a cry of horror when they began gliding in her direction.

This was unexpected. The spirits had never been provoked by a newborn before, but here they were heading straight towards Caitlin. Siobhan and Ava rushed to protect her but one of the spirits turned on them and screamed, "STAY!"

Panic erupted among the watching sorceresses, who were running in all directions. Entrapped by the melee, Caitlin could not escape. Where would she run to anyway? It did not look like anyone could hide from the Wraith. As they came closer, the crowd around her magically thinned, leaving her standing amidst a circle of ghostly sentries.

Caitlin tried hard to hold on to her composure but it was impossible. She was terrified. She would rather return to her earlier oblivion than hear them again, but it was not to be. She felt the cold building around her, stealing all the warmth and sucking all the light away. It took all the nascent courage she had to remain standing even though she was trembling like a leaf. She couldn't stop the tears streaming down her face. Her sight blurred and she could no longer see the other sorceresses.

From afar, she heard Siobhan's voice. "Remain calm, Caitlin. You are not alone." Ava's soft voice reached her too. Her friend and closest sister kept up a litany. "Be strong. Be strong. You can handle this."

But it was not to be. The gentle, supportive voices of her friends were soon buried by the harsher voices of the Wraith, which, once again, began in unison. *"Listen and listen well, Caitlin. A warning to you we bring..."* Caitlin drowned out the rest of their words, pressing her palms against her ears. She hoped and prayed that they would stop, that they would go away.

WHEN CAITLIN REGAINED HER SENSES, she didn't know if it had been hours or only a few minutes since her nightmare began. She saw her sisters staring at her, shock and curiosity reflecting in their expressions. Instead of the pride she had seen earlier, there was doubt. She saw the worried speculation in their eyes, for she had been marked by the Wraith, the sacred ones themselves.

Siobhan stepped forward. "What did they say to you?" she asked softly but firmly.

Caitlin realized the others hadn't heard the prophecy. She saw that Siobhan wasn't going to be satisfied unless she received an answer, but what should she say to her queen? Caitlin didn't fully understand the message of the Wraith yet. She wanted some time to absorb and understand what they were trying to tell her. She wasn't sure if she would ever be ready to accept their warning. She loved being a part of this clan. How could she betray them?

The spirits had either gone mad or had mistaken her for someone else. It had to be.

Everything was too raw and too personal to share with the others, even if she did call them sisters. Furthermore, she could see their distrust and doubt. Siobhan and Ava were the only ones still willing to give her a chance, but she couldn't bring herself to confide in them either. What if the warning of the spirits turned them against her too?

"My lady, I could not hear them. Words emerged from their mouths, true enough, but they did not make any sense to me," Caitlin whispered, stunned by her own duplicity. Ava, who stood right behind Siobhan, gave a start but managed to cover it up when Siobhan glanced behind. Caitlin realized Ava could sense she was lying but that she was giving her a chance.

Siobhan remained silent, as though weighing the impact of Caitlin's words. "It's understandable, I suppose. After all, you are a newborn. We shouldn't be in a hurry to forget that. I won't judge you, Caitlin. All of this is no fault of yours, but as soon as the words make sense, you need to come to me at once. Do you understand? I do need to know what the Wraith told you," Siobhan said urgently, glancing at the sorceress who stood behind her once again, but Ava's face was only an indistinct mask. Siobhan frowned but said nothing. Caitlin wondered if Siobhan knew that Ava was hiding the truth from her. She felt grateful to Ava for covering up her lie.

Before Caitlin had a chance to thank Ava, it was time for most of the sorceresses to leave, all except for the guardians, as Earth was their home and they would all soon disperse to their respective families. Caitlin watched with a mixture of awe and sadness as the only two sorceresses she felt a deep connection with departed to their respective abodes.

Siobhan stepped into a large revolving oval of light that appeared right in front of her. Caitlin could see bright sunshine on the other side even though the sky around her was already growing dark, heavy with the burden of night. Had she just caught a glimpse of Htrae? Would she ever be able to visit it?

Ava and a few other guardians had a long journey ahead of them, so were eager to get a head start. Ava had one last piece of advice for Caitlin. "Always remember that you are in possession of a unique gift—everlasting youth, an elixir humans are constantly in search of. You also possess immense power. You must protect your secret at all costs." Already deeply stung by the warning of the Wraith, Caitlin would go on to hold these words close to her heart and use them as a guiding principle in her interactions with humans.

Many of the other sorceresses followed Siobhan until only a handful of remained standing alongside Caitlin.

Trying to hide her misery, Caitlin looked around at the others hoping for a smile or some small show of solidarity, but now that Siobhan and Ava had left, the remaining guardians revealed their true colours. The twin masks of politeness and sisterhood were cast off. Being a guardian was a demanding job. The slightest chance of discovery and their families on Earth would be at risk. They had truly been happy and proud when Caitlin first emerged from the well, but now their feelings and expectations had undergone a sea of change. They did not trust her anymore.

"Siobhan is wrong about this one," said one guardian, rolling her amber eyes in Caitlin's direction. "She has stayed away from Earth for too long. Her judgment is off. She shouldn't let this new sorceress become a guardian."

A tempest raged inside her. Caitlin wanted to say she had a name they all gave her. She wanted to ask why they had forgotten it so quickly. But she kept her bitter thoughts to herself and stayed silent.

"What about Ava? She always supports Siobhan, right or wrong," claimed another. "Siobhan's right hand. It's as though the rest of us are useless." Caitlin realized Ava and Siobhan were facing a backlash for supporting her. She was filled with anguish to see their names being dragged through the mud right alongside her own.

Then someone addressed Caitlin directly, making her wish they had continued ignoring her. "You are an anomaly, someone who has induced the sentinels of death to break tradition, and we want to have nothing to do with you. Stay away from us, no matter what!"

The vitriolic looks the guardians threw her way hit Caitlin like ragged spikes tearing through her skin. She felt raw and exposed. Not everyone had misgivings about her. *Ava and Siobhan still believe in me,* she tried to convince herself.

But the worst was yet to come. Another opinion expressed without a thought to what it did to her. "I don't think Siobhan trusts her either. She is only waiting to see what the prophecy is. Until then, she cannot completely abandon this poor dear, can she?" claimed a guardian who had been envious of the attention Siobhan had showered on Caitlin.

Unfortunately, her bitter words did their work. Caitlin choked back a sob. A seed of doubt was sown in Caitlin's mind. Was Ava and Siobhan's support just a façade to hide their true intentions? Caitlin did not know what to believe anymore.

Resolve flowed through Caitlin. The prophecy of the Wraith would come to pass only if she digressed from her path, but she would stay true to her purpose. She would look at humans as vile and evil creatures and keep them at a distance. Her vulnerability made her cast a cloak of icy indifference, one that no man, no human, could cross. Or so she believed.

CHAPTER III

Mother, why did you hide the truth from Siobhan? Was it fear? You chose such a difficult path for yourself. Isolated by your own family, you distanced yourself from the only ones who could have offered you solace and comfort—humans. You were trying to be loyal to your sisters even if they were not loyal to you.
Talia

ＡLONE—CAITLIN

EVERY FEW YEARS, Ava made it a point to call upon Caitlin, no matter where Caitlin was. Siobhan would send her messages of love and support through Ava. Caitlin looked forward to seeing Ava and always received her with great warmth, but each time, an irrational fear haunted her. Would Ava bring up the prophecy? Would Ava try to persuade her to confide in Siobhan?

The poisonous comments of the guardians had long cast a shadow of doubt in Caitlin's mind, and even though she treasured Ava's friendship and Siobhan's concern, Caitlin still couldn't bring herself to open up to Ava. Caitlin badly wanted to be able to confide in her friend, but her own fears and doubts froze the words in her throat. Ava went away each time knowing that something lay unsaid between the two of them.

The truth was, Ava and Siobhan had grown to care for Caitlin, and it was only concern for her welfare that made Ava return again and again. Ava was a true friend and never divulged Caitlin's secret to Siobhan. Sometimes Caitlin saw the unspoken questions in Ava's eyes: *Why won't you tell Siobhan the truth? Why are you lying? Tell her what the spirits told you?* But Ava never voiced her concerns aloud. Year after year, decade after decade, it became easier for Caitlin to pretend there was no terrible secret gnawing at her heart day after day, sometimes almost paralyzing her with fear. She would never tell another soul what the spirits had warned her away from. She maintained only the barest and most fleeting of contact with humans, and she intended to keep it that way.

Caitlin stayed away from the gatherings and Siobhan never pulled her up for it. Who could blame Caitlin after what had happened at the first one? She may not recover from another confrontation with the spirits. Besides, Siobhan had never been able to patch things up between Caitlin and the rest of the guardians. Time had not changed them. Their hearts remained as cold as ever towards Caitlin.

Despite admonishments from Siobhan, the guardians, who were supposed to be the ones closest to Caitlin, treated her as tainted and broken. They saw her as a pariah, a castaway. It didn't matter that she hadn't committed any crime. She had been judged and found wanting. It suited them to forget her existence.

Caitlin's self-imposed exile from humans further isolated her.

It seemed that she could not escape many lifetimes of loneliness. Countless years passed, but thanks to her immortality, Caitlin did not age. She looked the same as she did when she first emerged from the Well of Creation.

Ava's past words of warning had chilled Caitlin to the bone. Because of the profound impact they'd had on her, she was determined never to become a tool for any human to exploit. Wherever she went, she focused on two things: ensuring that she blended into the background; and avoiding relationships of any sort.

As Caitlin learned to live with both the curse and blessings of immortality, she gained enough confidence to start exploring the planet, which held her in its sway from the moment she emerged from the holy water. She would not allow the Wraith or the guardians to take this joy away from her.

Every sorceress had a gift, and during her travels, Caitlin discovered hers. She had so much love to give and a heart so pure that no creature ever harmed her. Bereft of the company of her sisters and wary of humans, she found solace in the uncomplicated friendships of Earth's humble creatures. They did not scorn her like the guardians. Nor did they want anything from her like humans would if they knew her powers. They accepted her for who she was. The tiny creepy crawlies in the rain forests did not run from her. The fierce snow leopard prowling the slopes of the snow-covered peaks did not induce her to flee, nor did it seek to attack her. In her presence, even the lizards and snakes hiding in the cracks of rocks emerged. She petted crocodiles from the thickest swamps almost as though they were nothing but gentle Maltese dogs. In the magnificence and beauty of these creatures, Caitlin finally found a semblance of peace.

Time moved ahead in a relentless march, but to Caitlin, each day began to look the same. Revelation dawned that the more things changed, the more they remained constant. She had nothing to look forward to other than the occasional defiant supernatural she came across and had to deal with. Caitlin felt unfulfilled and yearned for something more. Was she denying the truth that was staring her in the face? Was it time for her *Rite of Passage* and for her to move on to the next world? Even after all this time, it still felt like her journey was incomplete.

Until Michael...

CHAPTER IV

Mother, was love worth risking it all for?
Despite all that happened, I suspect that if I ask you that question today
knowing what you do now, you may still answer in the affirmative. My
father, Michael, was truly a man worth loving and giving up everything
for.
Talia

FINDING LOVE—MICHAEL

MICHAEL LOVED the crowded town square of Jaesdan in the country of Masun. He was drawn to it because it was crammed with people of varied shapes and sizes from all walks of life. This was where the townsfolk gathered for all major or minor happenings in their lives, from theatrical performances and public speeches to sporting and ceremonial events. It was also where vendors peddled their wares, from jars of honey and spices to clay

vases, textiles, and figurines. Cobblers, potters and various arti-
sans jostled with each other, calling out loudly in an effort to
stand out. In the midst of all the hustle and bustle, Michael
felt alive.

Michael was a merchant who travelled frequently. He always
stayed for a while in the places he travelled to. There was nothing
calling him back to his home country of Aberevon except a pala-
tial but empty mansion. When in Aberevon, the silence in his
opulent house enveloped him and a fog of unhappy childhood
memories returned. That was why he always moved, never
staying long in one place.

When Michael was a teenager, both his father and mother
passed away within days of each other. Sympathetic visitors
bemoaned the matter of his being all alone in the world. He had
accepted their condolences graciously, never letting on the truth
that he had been alone for a very long time and was hard-pressed
to feel any grief for two strangers who had brought him into this
world but had never acknowledged him as their own, neither in
words nor actions. His parents had merely tolerated him because
he existed; yet Michael knew that he was luckier than most
children.

Standing over his parents' graves, he'd made himself a promise. He would always try to better the lot of the less fortunate children of the world.

Now it so happened that the market place of Jaesdan was also
refuge for all the homeless, abandoned and orphaned children of
the city. This was the place they came to spend the few pennies
they had, to peddle wares, or sometimes just to beg.

The sight of their tired, hungry and often desperate faces made
Michael's own dull and lonely childhood seem like a time of
rapture indeed. He couldn't abandon them. They became
Michael's salvation and he theirs.

Once, on a whim, Michael gathered all the children together.
They all sat at a roadside stall spooning steaming hot bowls of

frumenty, a thick wheat porridge boiled in a meat broth and seasoned with spices. The children had never eaten this delicacy before. They sat staring at Michael. Seeing him hurriedly digging into his food, Mehdi, the youngest, no longer needed an excuse and followed Michael's example. Barely had he spooned the first morsel into his mouth when his brother, Beni, followed him.

Since that day, Michael found himself heading to the market place every day around the same time. Some days it would be dried fruit and nuts and vegetable tagines. Other days it was a rice pudding. The children were an odd medley of varied ages, but at the mere sight of Michael, each and every face would light up.

The single hour soon began to stretch into a couple more, and Michael soon found himself engrossed in telling the children stories and teaching them the alphabet. His continued presence brought some stability to their lives. He also salvaged a little bit of their childhoods. They were a rough lot who had toughened up much earlier than they should have had to, but they opened their hearts to Michael. He knew this the moment they started calling him 'Baba', meaning father in the local dialect.

So what if he didn't have a family of his own. For now, Jaesdan was home and this city had had gifted him a beautiful family.

One early morning as Michael stepped out, the streets were unusually empty and quiet. It was so early that the first light of the sun had yet to break through the clouds. Michael loved the beauty of the dawn and decided to head out for a walk to be the first one in the market to see the stalls being laid out.

Absorbed in his own thoughts, Michael did not notice the subtle change in the aura around him. He came to an abrupt halt when he realized that someone was obstructing his way. The tall, well-built man blocking his path was less man and more some kind of creature. Time seemed to slow down and Michael noticed every little detail of the nightmarish stranger.

Dark, waist length dreadlocks covered the man-creature's head. Thick side-burns dominated its cruel face. Its mouth outlined by sharp, slightly curved teeth, was caked with spots of red, which Michael belatedly realized in horror was blood. Low-pitched, dangerous sounding growls emerged from *it*. The creature was bare from the waist upwards, but its disproportionately large and muscular torso was covered with long hair peppered with black and grey strands and matted with a mix of blood and mud. Its shoulders were hunched forward as if it was in extreme pain. Its long arms, also covered with hair, ended with sharp claws. The worst thing was that the creature's confused and unnaturally bloodshot eyes were trained on him—on Michael.

"Do you need help?" Michael croaked. Fear had almost stolen his voice. Even as he asked the question, he realized how absurd it was. The creature was not in need of any help; Michael was. The hour was still young and there was no one around. He was now in a lot of trouble. Furthermore, he was in an unfamiliar neighbour-hood, so even if anyone saw him, it was likely they would run for cover rather than foolishly try to come to his aid.

The creature obviously ignored his question. Michael was not even sure if it understood him. Instead, it took a couple of steps in Michael's direction. Michael knew he should do something—probably run or call out for help—but he instinctively sensed that the creature would be upon him before he would be able to do either.

Suddenly Michael was not alone any longer. A beautiful stranger stood between him and the creature. Caitlin stared eye to eye at the creature. As both man and creature, watched, Caitlin raised one hand and gently lowered the hood she wore over her head. Michael started in awe at the forest of blue that flowed right in front of his eyes. He had never seen hair of this rich hue before. It felt as though the sky was melting and flowing down in rivulets.

Michael was overawed, but seeing the blue haired lady had an even stranger effect on the creature. It lost most of its bluster. The bloodlust seemed to fade from its maniacal eyes. Michael avoided eye contact but was still determined to stand his ground.

Stubborn werexol, Caitlin murmured to herself. She had watched the werexol heading towards the human with dismay. Werexols were half man and half wolf. Shy and aggressive, these shape-shifting wolves were said to be descendants of a cursed king. This particular rabid creature must have got through a hole in the *Veil*, an invisible barrier that separated Earth from Htrae. The Heichi had fashioned the Veil as a shield between Earth and Htrae. The Veil was invincible only as long as good triumphed over evil on Earth. Bursts of hate, war, slavery, and other crimes against humanity caused sporadic gateways and passages to materialize in the shield, with supernaturals often making their way through. Caitlin had dealt with a few creatures in the past. She would deal with the werexol too.

Her concern lay in a different direction. She knew discretion was not possible at this stage. Her bachelor in a bind would learn her true identity and his memory would have to be wiped. Something urgent, curious and unfamiliar tugged at her heart at the mere thought that this handsome stranger wouldn't remember her anymore. *What is the matter with you?* she chided herself. *That is the way it is meant to be. Don't you supposedly hate humans anyway?* He was a stranger, but for some reason, she already knew more about him than she should. His eyes were bright with anxiety but she somehow knew that usually they shone with love and hope. The corners of his mouth were turned down with concern and displeasure at this moment, but they were typically set in a lopsided grin. His head, which he ducked in apprehension, was frequently thrown back in a deep-throated laugh.

"What are you doing?" Michael exclaimed, aghast at seeing her standing in front of him. His protective instincts kicked in and he snapped out of his dreamlike state. "It will hurt you," he shouted as he tried hard to pull Caitlin behind him. He didn't want her to die. His own death was acceptable to him, but not hers, not this beautiful stranger. As delicate as she looked, she hadn't budged an inch despite all his efforts to push her behind him. Instead, she gently removed his frantic hands from her arm and, turning her head towards him, smiled calmly. It was incandescent, imploring and mysterious all at once.

"Hello," she said. "I'm Caitlin, and I need your trust for just a little while."

His manners kicked in and he quickly muttered, "I am Michael." It seemed wrong to add, *I very badly don't want you to die.* The control and calmness in her voice disarmed him.

As if reading his mind, she smiled again and said, "I won't let anything happen to either of us. I've just found you. I'm not about to lose you. This man-creature is a werexol—not that you know what it means. I'm going to send it home, but for that, I need you to step back."

Ignoring Michael's confused expression, Caitlin turned her blue-eyed hypnotic gaze on the werexol. It seemed to resist her initially but gradually started to fall back. As soon as it bowed its head as though in submission, she raised her right hand towards it, her palm spread, whispering soft words in a strange language. The air around the werexol began whooshing and spiraling faster and faster until Michael could see the man-creature no more.

Michael began to feel slightly light-headed, so he closed his eyes to regain his balance. When he opened them again, the street was empty. The creature was gone, but so was the lady with hair like the sky. "Caitlin!" Michael screamed in panic. He dashed into the nearby alley to search for her, calling her name. Had the werexol snatched her and run away while his eyes were closed? She seemed more powerful than the creature; if so, where was she now? "Where are you? Please don't be gone. Don't leave," he shouted, his eyes darting around, but she was nowhere to be seen.

Despite her strong external shell, there was a vulnerability and childlike innocence about her that he found as appealing as her courage. The very thought of not seeing her again was unbearable. His search became even more frantic, and while he was relieved that there seemed to be no sign of the werexol, Caitlin had also completely vanished.

By the time a dejected Michael reached the town square, it was already late. The sun was still shining, but the passage of time was lost upon him. He'd spent hours searching for Caitlin but there was no sign of her or the werexol anywhere.

The regular gang of children waited for Michael under their usual haunt, a broad but bent ancient yew tree: Adil, Nora, Jasmin, Nabia, Hachim, Sophia, Beni and the youngest, Mehdi. Thankfully, they were safe. After failing to find Caitlin, Michael's next thought was for the safety of the children. He sighed with relief to find them safe and sound. They were crowded around his carved stone bench talking excitedly to someone he could not see. When he approached them, his mind still on Caitlin, they all rushed to him full of joy and excitement. It seemed they had a secret to share.

"We have a new friend, Baba. Come see," Adil shouted, catching sight of Michael.

"How nice," Michael mumbled back, his eyes fogging with unshed tears for no reason.

"She is very pretty," Beni whispered with a tinge of envy, for none of the girls he knew looked liked that. Their baba was a lucky man indeed. Michael finally looked at the newcomer in their midst. He rubbed his eyes in disbelief to see the friend they spoke of was none other than his rescuing angel, sitting there bold as you please surrounded by his children and smiling broadly.

"Where were you?" she asked, pretending to be angry at being kept waiting. "We have gone ahead and eaten without you, but your friends insisted on saving some honey cakes and stew for you. I hope you are hungry," she said, sounding happy.

She sounded like she cared for him a little bit, at least he hoped she did, for he had fallen—and fallen hard. Instead of the declarations of love that he wanted to spill out, all he said was, "It has been a long day. I could definitely do with something to eat." Beni looked quite disappointed. He seemed to have expected a more elaborate reply. Looking at the children, Michael grinned. "Thank you for leaving me something." Words of love could come later. For now, he needed a meal, otherwise he was going to faint, maybe in Caitlin's arms. Wouldn't Beni love that?

Anxious and not so soft whispers filled his ears. "Is she your girl, Baba?" It was Nabia who spoke this time. She looked slightly tearful as she looked at Caitlin laughing and joking with the others, not too sure if she wanted another to compete for Michael's love.

"What do you think? Is it okay for me to have a soft corner for her?" Michael asked Nabia. Nabia, the little mother of the group, chuckled because she could see this was much more than that. She was glad that Michael had finally found someone to love. She hoped Caitlin also felt the same way about him.

"Only if she makes you happy, Baba," was the little girl's reply. "Let me ask her," she added, and before Michael could stop her, she turned to Caitlin and said boldly, "Our friend really likes you. How do you feel about him?"

Michael was stunned. He hadn't expected such frankness from Nabia as she was as protective of him as she was of the other children. Even Adil fell into line when her dark eyes stared him down. Now her big, soulful eyes were fixed on Caitlin, waiting for an answer with great solemnity.

Caitlin said nothing. Michael and she had a connection that could not be ignored. So Caitlin said nothing to the little girl, but instead, rose from her place and entwined her fingers with Michael's. He had been given an answer. His face split into a happy grin. The children erupted into shouts and yells. It was a mad scene but after a long, long time, Caitlin was deliriously happy and didn't mind the noise in the least.

CHAPTER V

Mother and Father, I see it now. You were meant to find each other and be together. Nothing, least of all an ancient prophecy or the curse of immortality, could keep you apart. But why is life always about choices? As we go one way, we have to forgo the other. When you chose my father, you had to leave your sisters behind—even the ones you cared so deeply about.

Talia

THE SECRET MEDALLION—CAITLIN AND NABIA

MICHAEL AND CAITLIN were married with the children bearing witness. Before they knew it, their last day in Masun had arrived. They would be taking a ferry across the Strait of Njoria from the port of Zabat to start their journey to Aberevon, Michael's home and now Caitlin's. Their journey to Zabat from Jaesdan had taken a couple days. The children had accompanied them for a small leg of it, but now the ferry would take the newlyweds onwards to Algeciras, and then they would travel to Aberevon.

As Caitlin stood waiting for Michael, a cold easterly wind blew tendrils of her hair onto her face. Pierced stones littered the quay at regular distances to provide mooring to the boats and ferries. A fierce storm could wrench at a ship, but would it still hold? What would happen to her and Michael if Siobhan learned the truth? Would they be able to weather that storm?

Caitlin's medallion was her last link to Ava, Siobhan and the Heichi. It was a special gift from Siobhan to her. As far as Caitlin knew, no other guardian had ever received such a gift. She had told Michael everything about herself, even the prophecy of the Wraith. Michael knew everything there was to know about Caitlin. She was an immortal sorceress tainted by an ugly prophecy, but he still loved her. Nothing could change that. The medallion was the only thing she held back on.

CAITLIN REMEMBERED her last interaction with Siobhan before the queen returned to Htrae. The Wraith had gone leaving Caitlin in shambles. She had been lost, confused and heartbroken. She had been looking forward to her new life but the Wraith had changed everything. As she wallowed in self-pity and misery, a hand tapped her shoulder. She turned around and found herself looking into Siobhan's eyes, golden with flecks of brown.

"Caitlin," Siobhan had said solemnly, her voice filled with empathy and sorrow. "I am so sorry for what happened to you here today. I want nothing more than to keep you close, but I have to say goodbye. There are some problems in Htrae that need attention. Ava, too, has to return to Calabrigh, her home. You are not alone. Your guardian sisters surround you," she had said. "Wear this medallion at all times. It is a special gift for you. It has special powers. None of the other guardians have a medallion like this. I think you will need it to protect you. It will link you to Ava. Never part with it. Hold it tight in your palm if you are in trouble. Let it grow as warm as fire to your touch and Ava will know that you need her even though there are thousands of miles between the two of you." Saying this, Siobhan had slipped a simple medallion bearing the triquetra symbol around Caitlin's neck, gesturing to Ava that it was her turn to bid the new guardian farewell.

"Goodbye, Caitlin. Reach out to me if you need me. Call me and I will come to you; don't worry." It was once again Ava's eyes that spoke volumes; they were trusting but all seeing. *I know you lied to Siobhan*, they seemed to say, *but you must have a reason. I hope I am not wrong about you.* As Siobhan had approached, Ava looked away, deliberately breaking eye contact with Caitlin almost as if she'd feared Siobhan would read her mind and learn the truth.

AS THE NEWLYWEDS and the children said their final tearful farewells, Caitlin slipped the medallion in the hands of Nabia. Had she done the right thing by giving the medallion away? Yes, she had, because while the medallion was a way for her to call for help, it was also a beacon that could lead the Heichi to her. Ava knew what the prophecy was, Caitlin was sure of it. She had seen both the understanding and sorrow in her eyes. If she told Siobhan the truth, her relationship with Michael would be at risk. Michael was Caitlin's anchor; she couldn't imagine a life without him. For this reason, she knew she was doing the right thing.

"Nabia, you are wise beyond your years. I have watched how you care for the younger ones better than a mother would her own child. I want to tell you something about myself, a secret which only your baba knows, but you must promise to tell no one," said Caitlin.

"What great secret is this, Ommah? I will tell no one."

Reassured, Caitlin said, "I am not just an ordinary woman. I am an enchantress." Seeing the fear and shock on Nabia's face, Caitlin added, "But there is nothing to be afraid of. I would never hurt any of you. I love all of you. I hope you know that. Do you trust me, Nabia?"

"You are a Sahira, an enchantress?" Nabia asked, her eyes as round as saucers and her hand shaking, but she did not flee. Nabia appeared to be deep in thought for a while but then finally she said, "I trust Sahira because Baba trusts you."

Caitlin took that as a sign that Nabia accepted what she was trying to tell her. Caitlin's relief was palpable. She continued, "I know we are leaving Jaesdan but Michael, your baba, will always stay in touch with you. I also know that when he fails to visit, some of you are sure to visit him. You will ensure that your baba is okay even when I am not around, which is why is I need to entrust something important to your care. If a day comes when you feel that Baba is in trouble, use this." Caitlin gave Nabia the medallion. "Look after this for me, Nabia," she pleaded. "I have a sister; her name is Ava. This medallion will act as a guide to help her reach you, but only when you need her. Tell her your worry. She will help."

A puzzled Nabia asked, "Won't it be better off with you? You will be with Michael all the time."

"I cannot keep it with me because my family does not know about Michael. They would never approve. They may try to separate the two of us. Ava and the rest of my family must not find me right now. I have to keep this medallion far from me because when it is with me, it acts like a beacon for her to find me. I do not have anyone else to turn to. Will you keep my secret?" asked Caitlin.

"Yes," said Nabia with determination. She would do anything to bring a smile back to this beautiful lady's face. She must help them. After all, Michael had done so much for them. They were orphans who he had treated like family. He had given them food and shelter, but more than that, he had given them love and friendship. Anything she could do to repay the debt would never be enough.

"You have a strange family, Ommah Sahira. If they don't come to celebrate your happiness, what makes you think they will come when there is trouble?"

Caitlin smiled. Nabia was now calling her *Mother Enchantress*. "You are indeed wise, Nabia. I have chosen the right custodian for the medallion. To answer your question, yes, they will come; I am sure. I have my reasons for hiding Michael from them, but when in trouble, I know Ava will come to our aid. She does not judge."

"I will not ask what happened to separate you from your sister. Don't worry, for you also have another family. Baba and us, we are your family too, aren't we?" Nabia asked. She giggled. "And one day, you will have children of your own. I will keep this safe for your family just in case, but I hope we never need to use it."

Nabia's thought had such a beautiful ring to it. "I hope we don't need it either," Caitlin whispered. Michael, and now Nabia, had mentioned children. Someday she would love to have her own family. Would such a reality be possible, or would the Wraith claim her first?

"In case you do need help, how does the medallion work?" asked Nabia.

"You need to clasp it in your palm tightly. When it feels hot, very hot, it means the magic is at work," she said. "Don't worry; it won't hurt you," she added, seeing the crease of worry on Nabia's forehead.

"I know, Ommah Sahira. You would never hurt me," said Nabia. "But I am just a girl. Will I be able to do what you ask of me? What if I let you down?" Concern laced her voice.

"Impossible!" exclaimed Caitlin. "You don't even know what you children and Michael have done for me. I had no one. I was an outcast in my own family, but you all took me in and gave me love and a family. No, you could never let me down."

CHAPTER VI

The two of you were my family. Together you taught me everything I know and gave me all the skills that would one day help me survive, and for that, I am grateful. Above all, you gave me love.
Talia

YEARS WENT BY. Theirs was a happy household filled with laughter and harmony. Caitlin was living a dream she hadn't ever imagined possible. Life was perfect until Caitlin and Michael learned they would soon be welcoming a baby into their lives. Michael was ecstatic. His thoughts were of the giggles and laughter that would fill their house. He desperately missed the children of Jaesdan. He knew they had played an important role in bringing Caitlin into his life. Before the two of them had left for Aberevon, he'd made sure they were taken care of, but that didn't mean he missed them any less. The very thought of having his own child, maybe a little girl with Caitlin's big eyes and cerulean blue hair, made him a very happy man. Caitlin, on the other hand, felt the first stirring of fear within her. The warnings of the Wraith echoed in her mind. But Michael's happiness and excitement was so very endearing that she cast away her anxieties for a while. Michael had always wanted a daughter, even before he and Caitlin were married. *I hope we have a girl*, he had said. *If you haven't a name in mind, I would like to call her Talia, and I hope she is just like you—perfect.* However, any daughters born of a union between a sorceress and a human would be half blood, supernatural with the full power of Caitlin's Heichi ancestors. Only the daughters inherited the power; any sons would be mortal.

WHEN A BABY GIRL WAS BORN, Caitlin worried incessantly. She had never cared for an infant before. She had never even experienced childhood. Not the best qualifications for her to make an adequate mother to a half blood. However, Michael's reassurances gradually soothed Caitlin and she began to dream of a normal life for her newborn daughter, Talia. Maybe their Heichian heritage would ensure Talia would always be strong and independent. If Michael's perceptive nature and aura were ingrained in Talia, she would never go wrong. Caitlin hoped that her own powers and fortitude would play a part in becoming Talia's shield against the shadows and threats that inherently flawed the life of a sorceress.

Michael knew a day might come when their child would be hunted or chased for her power. He wanted Talia to be prepared for any unknown danger, but Caitlin felt otherwise. Her own past had embittered her and taught her that power did not assure happiness. She argued that Talia must be allowed to enjoy her childhood, have a chance to grow into her own destiny and to find her own way, for this was a joy that Caitlin never had.

Michael sensed there was something else bothering Caitlin, some unknown fear that she refused to share with him. Denying Talia her birthright was about more than her having a normal childhood. All he told Caitlin was, "Her powers would allow her to protect herself like you can, but if she can't have that, you must make her strong both in mind and body. Trouble may find her someday. Shouldn't our girl be ready for it?"

"I will do my best but I need you to promise me something," Caitlin said.

"Just say the words."

"You will always watch out for her if anything—"

"Shhh," said Michael. "Don't even think about saying something like that." Michael picked up little Talia and kissed her forehead. "I will always watch out for our little girl whatever the cost." And with that, ready or not, Talia's tutelage under Caitlin started in earnest even though she was little more than a toddler.

When Michael returned home after his travels, Talia would run to him eager to show off the new moves she had learned. Be it the sword or archery, or any other weapon at her disposal, Caitlin intended for Talia to be well versed.

On occasion, when Caitlin pushed Talia to the boundaries of her endurance, Talia's powers often broke through, thrusting back in return. Whenever Talia instinctively used her powers, Caitlin's only focus would be on diffusing her fears and bringing matters to a normal keel as soon as possible. If Caitlin was injured by the sheer brute force of her daughter's powers, she hid it from a worried Talia and reassured an apprehensive Michael.

Just like her parents, Talia was fond of animals. Caitlin would often take her to the stables, whispering horse wisdom into her daughter's ear. "All horses really need is hay, water, good grooming and love. If you add carrots and sugar cubes as a treat, your horse will always welcome you."

Under her mother's able tutelage, Talia mastered her equestrian skills by the young age of six. On her seventh birthday, she was gifted a beautiful mountain pony. Much to their amusement, Talia named her pony Liata, an anagram of her own name.

Like her mother, Talia learned to see beauty in all creatures of nature. Caitlin sensed that Talia had the same magic in her soul, that divine part of her that would always draw creatures wild or tame towards her. But little Talia remained oblivious to her magical ancestry and just enjoyed the special time with her mother.

Michael was right in sensing Caitlin's reluctance to use magic. The truth was that Caitlin feared the use of magic would help the Heichi find her. Since committing to Michael, she hadn't let a single spell flow through her hands, nor had she uttered a word of magic.

In her mind, she was no longer a guardian, only a wife and a mother. She blamed the Wraith for forcing her to choose. But every time she looked at Michael and Talia, she knew she had made the right choice by giving away Siobhan's medallion, severing her last link with the Heichi.

The rituals and powers of a sorceress remained hidden from Talia, who was never given reason by either of her parents to believe that she was anything other than an ordinary girl, nothing more than human. But sorceresses were not human, so Caitlin had one constant message for Talia: "Be careful who you trust and also who you give your love to." Talia may not have known she was a sorceress, but Caitlin feared that the greedy humans would learn of Talia's aberration and try to manipulate her for it.

CHAPTER VII

Mother and Father, you were my family and Joshua was my sun. He was my world. You gave me love but Joshua taught me how to love.
Talia

ALIA'S KNIGHT—JOSHUA

A YEAR LATER, when they welcomed a delightful baby boy into their family, little Talia was quick to christen him Joshua, and with Michael not having the heart to disappoint his daughter, the name stuck.

As an older sibling, Talia could have resented the interloper on her parents' affections, but she displayed no signs of any ill will towards her brother. On the contrary, from the moment she set her eyes on Joshua, she loved him with all her heart. She was forever by Caitlin's side assisting her in caring for the baby and cooing him to sleep.

Joshua proved himself to be a playful but good-natured boy. He was always chasing after something, and when the inevitable happened and he hurt himself, it was always his sister he would run to. Every time Joshua stepped into the garden, Talia would be ready and waiting to tend to his scrapes and bruises.

Talia would tell Joshua stories of knights, their brave steeds, and terrible monstrous dragons. Joshua would then take his little wooden spear and attempt to impale a mighty dragon, which was actually a fluffy pillow. When the scattered feathers caused Caitlin much dismay, Talia and Joshua would have no choice but to hide to escape her wrath. Talia took to calling Joshua her 'knight' even though she was the one always rescuing him. His little face would glow with pride and he would manfully puff his chest and cast a plump arm around her as though in protection. Where Talia went, on tubby little legs Joshua would follow. Seeing how inseparable the two of them were, Caitlin often lovingly referred to Joshua as Talia's shadow.

Joshua and Talia had a little game between them. As soon as he saw his sister, the little boy would start spinning. Round and round he would go and the only way to make him stop was for Talia to hug him. This was Joshua's favourite game, which he insisted on playing only with Talia and no other. A typical conversation between brother and sister went like this:

"What are you doing, Joshua?" Talia would say, trying to feign exasperation.

"I am busy; can't you see?" he would reply.

"Busy how? You don't seem to be doing much," she would say in turn.

"I am going around the world on my dragon. The whole world. Woohoo! Woohoo!" he would say.

The little boy would whirl and swivel, not stopping until his sister enveloped him in a great big hug.

Caitlin felt extremely protective of Joshua, for he was not a half blood like Talia. The male children of the Heichi sorceresses were devoid of magical ability. They were fully mortal, and to them, enchantments and spells were akin to poison. In a way, they were even more fragile than humans because not only did they not have any powers, but even good magic was damaging to them.

The overwhelming rush of maternal instincts for her human child overpowered Caitlin with guilt. It wasn't right to differentiate between her two children. Was she being tougher on Talia because the child was supernatural like her? Did she have unreasonable expectations from her daughter? Her guilt made her suppress her show of affection for Joshua. She did not want her daughter to feel ignored, so Caitlin forced herself to keep her son at arms' length, never hugging or cuddling him. But Joshua didn't notice Caitlin's carefully cultivated reserve because he adored his sister. She was perfect and she was his. She made him feel safe.

Despite these hiccups in her life, Caitlin was proud of her little family. Michael still travelled, but things were different now. His life was teeming with joy and he no longer had any unhappy memories to run away from. He would return to home and hearth as quickly as time and travel permitted. Whenever Michael visited Jaesdan, he brought back news of their little friends, who were not so little any more.

CHAPTER VIII

"Listen and listen well, Caitlin. A warning to you we bring. Hear our voices and not your heart, for nothing but disaster it will bring. A man will come into your life when you expect not, and things will never be the same. For the sake of the child born of this union, you will your family betray. Be warned and be wise and from him stay away."

This was the prophecy of the Wraith, which ruined your life and ours too, Mother. You found solace in Father's love for a while, but when your past came back to haunt you, instead of standing tall and cohesive, you broke away from us. No longer a unit, we splintered apart until there was nothing left to be broken.

Talia

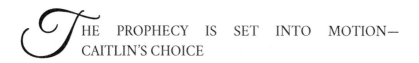

THE PROPHECY IS SET INTO MOTION— CAITLIN'S CHOICE

ONE FINE AUTUMN MORNING, Caitlin awoke in cold sweat. An ominous feeling besieged her. She hoped that it was temporary and would pass in the brightness of the day. But even as she watched the leaves fall from the trees, the words of the Wraith came back to haunt her. This time she could not shut them out.

Caitlin looked at her innocent children. She was blessed. The two of them asked for nothing as long as they had each other. But her past was no longer a threat far beyond the horizon. It was a dark cloud hovering over them. If anything happened to them, she would never be able to forgive herself.

Obsessed by the prophecy, Caitlin began to fret. Michael knew that something was troubling her but she refused to confide in him. What would she tell him? What would he do? She never should have followed her heart. Love had made her weak and unable to make the sacrifice of walking away from Michael, but now. Now it was time to put her family's welfare before her own selfish needs.

Caitlin finally saw a way out of her torment. She was born a guardian and it was now time to don that mantle again. She had to protect her little family. She and the cursed child must be separated from each other. If they were not together, the prophecy could not come to pass.

But how does a mother choose? Choosing between her children seemed implausible and unthinkable, but for the sake of her family, she had to do it. She had to know which child lived under the shadow of the curse.

In little Joshua, who was so innocent and without guile, Caitlin saw Michael and the peace and calm he brought to her life. In Talia, she saw an image of herself, the strength, the promise of power, and unfortunately, the pain it could bring. Talia was the half blood; the prophecy predicting Caitlin would betray the Heichi on account of her child had to be related to Talia.

The blood of the Heichi flowed in Talia's veins, which meant she must be strong. Caitlin had seen glimpses of her daughter's power often enough, even if Talia didn't know her own strength.

Joshua, on the other hand, was mortal. He needed his mother's magic.

After dwelling on her decision and changing her mind a thousand times, Caitlin hastily bundled up Joshua one night and fled. She left no note, no message. Separating herself from Talia to protect them all, Caitlin's intentions were noble. She knew there could be no long drawn goodbyes else her courage would fail her.

The next morning, Talia and Michael awoke to a world without Caitlin and Joshua. It was as if they had never existed. Any reminder of them had been ruthlessly destroyed or hidden by Caitlin. With her cowardice, Caitlin thus set into motion that which she had fought tooth and nail to avoid. She broke Michael's heart, inadvertently setting the prophecy in motion.

TALIA AND MICHAEL took this blow differently. Michael was stoic for a few days, thinking that Caitlin wouldn't be able to stay away. He had always believed that their love would overcome Caitlin's fears, but he hadn't accounted for a mother's anxiety for her children or a wife's love for her husband. Caitlin genuinely believed that she was protecting them all by running away. As time went by with no sign of Caitlin or Joshua, Michael got frantic when he realized they were not coming back.

Talia's reaction had been more realistic. She ventured as far as she could without worrying Michael, making enquires of strangers: *"Has anyone seen a woman and a small boy?"* Sheer waiting would have driven her mad. But when all her efforts turned up nothing, she realized no one had taken them forcibly. Her mother just did not intend to be found.

Talia convinced herself that her mother and Joshua would return in their own time, but she needed something to hold on to, a talisman to believe in a happily ever after. She turned the house upside down until she found one last toy of Joshua's that had escaped Caitlin's harsh spring-cleaning. It was a clay horse. Clutching the little horse in her hands, Talia locked herself in her room, weeping buckets for days and nights until she had no more tears to shed.

When Talia finally emerged, she was no longer a child but the woman of the house. She had a father to care for and a household to manage. The innocent child of just a few days earlier was gone forever.

CHAPTER IX

Wasn't being king of Aberevon enough for Damien? Why did he want the world? Why did he need my family to fulfil his greedy dreams? The first crack in our family appeared when my mother disappeared with Joshua. My father and I would have eventually found her, but King Damien made sure that what was broken could never be joined.
Talia

ESTINED TO BE KING—DAMIEN

KING DAMIEN HAD a sneaky feeling that the people of Aberevon were compelled to curtsy and bow to him due to the presence of his guards and their sharp spears. He was their lord and master; they owed him their fealty. If they couldn't give him their love, at least he had their fear. It was not long since he had usurped the throne after killing his adoptive father. That man had taught him one valuable lesson: There was no discipline without misery and dashed hopes. Lack of fear was a perfect scenario for rebellion. A suppressed person always falls in line; Damien's own childhood experiences taught him that.

From the day the sorceress Ava put him in her arms, the queen of Aberevon loved Damien as her own. His father, on the other hand, could never accept a child not of his flesh and blood. He detested Damien on sight. "We have to christen you, it seems," the king of Aberevon announced, looking at him.

"What do you mean?" Damien asked respectfully.

"Give you a name, you fool," the king explained irritably.

"What for?" he said. "I already have a name. It is Damien. I shall be known by this name and no other." The king looked at the little boy with grudging respect. Maybe he was not as spineless as he believed. It was going to be even more fun to break him.

Damien sensed the king's dark thoughts but he was not afraid. Looking at his new father, he realized that humans were as dangerous as supernaturals. No matter. His 'father' was a minor inconvenience who could be crushed like an insect at the right time, just like the giants had almost crushed him.

Damien was only six years old when the sorceress Ava travelled with him through the mantle of time and taken him to Aberevon. He was always a fragile child, so this free falling through time further impacted his health. To the king, he was a black mark on their ancestral legacy of warriors. The king was always impatiently waiting for the day his 'son' would give in to his frequent bouts of illness.

It was Damien's ill fate that the benevolent and caring queen passed away just two years after taking him in, leaving eight-year-old Damien as the ward of the brutish and vicious king. Her presence may have brought out the goodness in him, it may have saved him, but without her, the darkness within Damien would only grow stronger.

Before his courtiers, the king was an attentive father, instructing Damien in matters of the state and even letting him participate at court. When they were alone, the king was a different man, one who spared no opportunity to humiliate Damien. He taunted him about his past, his puny build, anything and everything he saw as a weakness.

Damien never said a word. He allowed the king's harsh words to wash over him. He used them to help him focus on the future. The king would also thrash the boy at the slightest provocation while being careful not to mark him in any way. Damien stoically took the torture, thinking of it as the price he had to pay to become king. He hated his *father* for the way he tortured him. He hated his mother for dying on him. He hated Ava for forsaking him. One day, he would get his vengeance.

As if in rebellion, Damien survived, growing to be tall and slender with long dark hair that fell below his shoulders. He was extremely pale but for his eyes, which blazed with such intelligence. The antithesis of Damien in looks, the king's hate towards his adoptive son grew in leaps and bounds every day. The king had a dark, fierce face with glittering eyes that were quick to reflect his anger. He wore his muscled, scarred chest and broken bones with the pride of a seasoned warrior. He couldn't understand or accept Damien's flawless and graceful features or his slender limbs. He was a hearty man, well built with massive shoulders and beefy arms, and in his eyes, Damien was still a puny, good-for-nothing child.

The king wasn't discreet in his search for a worthy heir among nephews and far-flung cousins. Damien may have been weak, but he was not stupid. He knew that an heir would turn up sooner or later, an encroacher to his throne. Which fool would walk away from so rich a bounty and a prosperous kingdom as Aberevon handed over to them on a platter?

Damien decided it was time to retire his father before it was too late. It was time to get his revenge.

As predicted, the king's cruelty only fanned the spark of evil within Damien into a full-blown flame. As Damien grew older, viciousness and savagery became second nature to him. He didn't see things as black, white or grey, only the way he wanted. What Damien needed, Damien had to get, no matter the price others had to pay for it. He had learned from the best.

The king's unabashed smugness made him oblivious to the feral glint and the growing menace lurking in Damien's eyes, otherwise he would have been more wary of him. Habitually accustomed to baiting and ill-treating Damien, he didn't realize that the boy was now strong enough to fight him and smart enough to plot against him.

Ava had wanted Damien to experience love, power, and happiness in human measures, but he had seen too much of the supernatural and the might it could wield over mankind. He wanted revenge. He coveted forever and he craved immortality. He wanted the throne.

The king would not have been impressed to know that his hated son had successfully followed in his steps and had, in fact, overtaken him in machinations and intrigue. It definitely wouldn't have thrilled the king to realise that he would be the very first victim of Damien's active foray into violence. It was a handy tumble down the palace stairs, a result of Damien's well-placed foot, that put an end to the king's hunt for a successor and to his life.

For the embittered and jaded people of Aberevon, things didn't change much because one cruel king had replaced another. They didn't really care how the old king had died. They didn't know that Damien's penchant for violence would make their old king seem positively benign.

The king's death cleared the way for Damien to take his place. Damien had taken his own destiny in his hands. He was taking no chances. No one would stand in his way, even if that someone were his own father.

Damien saw himself as strong and powerful, but although he

had a mind capable of the craftiest and calculating plots, intrigues and machinations, his body could never quite keep up.

Ava had tried to use magic to wipe his memory, but the truth was that Damien's brain had always been wired differently. Ava had failed in expunging all traces of the Purge, his family, and even their flight through the curvature of space.

Physicians from around the world had tried to restore his health since childhood at the behest of the queen, his adoptive mother, but failed to find either a cause or a remedy for the ailments and the feeling of malaise that constantly plagued him.

Damien knew that if he had to take his rightful place in the world, the little matter of his own fragile constitution had to be taken care of. Nothing could stand in his way.

Every time the imprint of the soulful hazel eyes of Ava impinged on his memory, Damien silently cursed her for the state of his health and his uncertain future. Damien's faded memory of the time he once belonged to reinforced his suspicion that his flaky and frail health was the result of magic. He feared he would not find the answers he sought amongst the healers. The vestiges of his past memories convinced him that only Ava or her sisters could give him eternal life and the health he craved.

Damien remembered what Ava had unwittingly told him. There were others like her. Perhaps they could cure him and make him just like them. Damien knew that he had to find Ava, or at least one of her sisters, thus becoming very dangerous to the guardian sorceresses on Earth, including Caitlin.

CHAPTER X

Whom were you hiding from, Mother? Was it your own fears, or the sense of the inevitable? Watch out; they are coming for you and Joshua.
Talia

THE HUNT FOR A SORCERESS—GARCIA AND THE HISTORIAN LUIGI

DAMIEN NEVER SAW Ava again after she left him at Aberevon. She didn't visit him once. All that talk about caring for him had been utter rubbish and a waste of words. Even though she had told him he would never return, he felt she should have done so anyway. She was an immortal, which meant she still lived somewhere on Earth, so he would find her. If not her, another of her kind, the sisters she spoke of with so much love. Yes, he was going to find himself his very own sorceress.

Damien was quite unaware that the very war that had destroyed his family had forced the supernaturals to create a magical realm of their own so as to give peace on Earth a chance. But the Heichi were still not safe from him, for unfortunately, the guardian sorceresses still remained on Earth, and with his limited knowledge, Damien was a danger to them all. It was beneficial to the lives of his men that Damien was quite ignorant of the fact that until almost a year ago, a Heichi sorceress had lived in his own domain. But now Caitlin had abandoned Aberevon and there were no Heichi sorceresses in sight.

Damien put his father's bookish and priggish scholars, historians and librarians to work amongst the treasured and voluminous tomes of the citadel library. He had two simple wishes: to be the strongest and most powerful man of that time; and to live forever.

The men searched and searched at the pain of death, but no tome or manuscript documented the most powerful secrets, or even the existence of the Heichi. When Damien saw doubt in their eyes and the conviction that he was mad for believing in things like sorceresses, he executed ten of them. Satisfied that the remaining ten were now terrified enough and determined to find a sorceress, he sent them out to the farthest corners of the world, each accompanied by one of his hunters.

The king's hunters were a special troop of elite soldiers who were the best trackers and spies from all over the world. They worked for King Damien because he appreciated their worth and paid them well. To him, they were more valuable than his ministers, who did nothing but grow fat and rich. The hunters were not the tallest, nor the strongest, but they had an amazing sense of direction, a way to extract information and to unearth clues where there were none.

The best man in his employ was a swarthy fellow called Garcia. He was short and burly, and if you missed the wicked and manipulative gleam in his eyes, he appeared harmless. Many a quarry of Damien's had been defeated because they underestimated Garcia and his hunting skills.

The wisdom and secrets of the past could not be easily revealed, and only three historians survived. The laziest one did not take any risks and was conniving enough to mislead the hunter accompanying him. He could not fool King Damien. No sooner had they returned than he summarily had them executed. The other two were a pair of brothers, Luigi and Marco. Luigi, the younger and shrewder of the two, was determined to save his own life and that of his brother. Marco, the wiser of the two, was a scholar who studied ancient religions. He volunteered to go Zedresh, hoping that amidst the monasteries and temples, some secrets would reveal themselves.

Luigi and Garcia retained Aberevon and Masun for sorceress hunting. The terror of Garcia spurred Luigi to explore corners and ruins that no one had attempted before. By now, Garcia was well versed in the king's ways. He knew his life and that of his brother were on the line. *Find a sorceress or die.*

Finally, on an island called Neptheas in the Sea of Rinai off the Aberevon mainland, Garcia and Luigi discovered some ancient texts lending credence to King Damien's rant about the Heichi sorceresses.

"The king was right," said Luigi to Garcia. "A long time ago, such sorceresses walked the Earth in large numbers along with other supernatural creatures."

"I thought the king had sent us on a wild goose chase," exclaimed Garcia. "So where do we find them?" he asked eagerly. The two of them had been on the road for almost a year and Garcia very badly wanted to head home to his beautiful wife and daughter.

Luigi was still poring over the fragile scroll. He looked up, disappointment ridden over his face. "There is mention of a great war between humans and supernaturals. After this war, the sorceresses seem to have disappeared from the face of the Earth. There were other creatures that disappeared too. Can you believe that even dragons, wolfmen and giants existed a long time ago?

Do you think they were all wiped out?" he asked, anxiety under-lying his voice. Garcia knew that it was not the fear of unknown creatures that caused the tremor in Luigi's voice but dread of King Damien. Without a sorceress to present to their king, they were only risking their heads. Damien did not need affirmation. He knew he was right. He wanted a sorceress—a living, breathing sorceress.

"What do we do?" asked Luigi. The journey had forged an unlikely partnership between the two men. If they went back empty handed, they would be executed, no questions asked.

"We keep searching," replied Garcia. "We have explored the east, the west and the south of this continent. I think instead of moving further south towards Masun, we should cross Aberevon and head north."

"Return all the way back?" asked Luigi. "That is quite a gamble," he said quietly.

"Something tells me that we should head north. I don't have a reason, but my instincts have never let me down so far," said Garcia. "Look, Luigi, if you have a compulsion to go south, I won't stop you. I trust you," he laughed. "A first for me. We split up and we look for this sorceress."

Luigi stared at Garcia in astonishment. He had always treated Garcia as little more than a thug. He swallowed the lump of guilt that rose in his throat. His voice gruff, he said, "No, let's stick together. We will go north but let us bypass Aberevon. I have a bad feeling that if we return empty handed, we will not live to see another day."

The two were silent for a while. It was a lot to absorb—the discovery of the scroll, the fear for their lives, and the long journey that lay ahead of them.

∼

CAITLIN CHOSE SZEVACI, as far north from Aberevon as she could

go as home for her and Joshua. It had a desolate landscape dominated by imposing geographic boundaries with mountains on all
four sides. The mountainous terrain gradually subsided to make
way for the waters of fast flowing icy rivers that moved rapidly to
the nearby plains. At the foot of the mountains, which stretched
from the northwest to the southeast in an arc, lay a large fragment
of forested area. Caitlin knew they would be safe in a habitat
teeming with brown bears, wolves, chamois and lynxes. No
animal ever harmed her; they always saw her as a friend.

Unlike Talia, Joshua was terrified of animals, especially the
ones in the wilderness, so the animals gave their home a wide
berth, but Caitlin still hoped the animals would keep other
dangers at bay. What about the Wraith? Nothing could keep them
away. The spirits of the Heichi sorceresses would probably scare
away all her animal protectors with one single hoarse whisper.
She had to avoid thinking about them and just hope for the best.

Joshua, unaware of his mother's worries and hopes, clung to
Caitlin, terrified of the isolation and bleakness surrounding him,
desperately missing Talia. Even the trout in the river, arcing their
bodies as they performed a merry dance of their own, couldn't
distract him from the strange swirls and twists in the grey mist
around them.

Joshua took to sitting on the embankment by the river for
hours on end, its rough trails covered with broken boughs
watching the wild waters rush by. Staring at the water, tears blur-
ring his eyes, he imagined Talia's sweet face smiling at him. He
never went far away from his mother, though. Caitlin's repeated
pleas and entreaties to return home for supper made from the
door of their home adjacent to the river would reluctantly break
through his reverie and pull him back to their little cottage.

CHAPTER XI

If only we had stayed together. If only I had been with you and Joshua. The torture Damien put you through must have been horrible, but imagining your pain was much worse. Maybe the feeling of helplessness I felt wouldn't be so great if I had been there to share your torment and heartache.

Talia

CAPTURED—CAITLIN AND JOSHUA

CAITLIN DID NOT KNOW what or whom she had fled from. Was it herself she feared? The prophecy had spoken about her perfidy, but she could never imagine letting Siobhan down or betraying Ava's trust. It was true that she had cast off her Heichi vows the day she took Michael's hand, but she had never gone against the Heichi in any way, and she never would.

Almost two years had passed and Joshua was now almost

seven years old. But despite the passage of time, his yearning for home hadn't dampened in the least. His homesick eyes gnawed at her, and to her horror, Caitlin often felt her own resolve to stay away weaken. *Don't forget the prophecy*, she would tell herself in an attempt to stem the revolt rising within her. *Joshua wants to return home, as do I, but we can't; we just can't. It isn't safe.*

Caitlin had no choice but to suppress the deep ache of longing to see the precious faces of Joshua's father and sister, but since Szevaci was isolated and free of prying eyes, there amidst the isolation, Caitlin found a degree of solace by surrendering to her senses and becoming one with nature once again as she had been a long time ago before Michael.

In Aberevon, she had been careful to always cover her beautiful hair, but even though she still used no magic, she had taken to leaving her blue locks wild and free once again. It reminded her of who she was and the promise of loyalty to her clan and erstwhile sisters. She could never forget Michael and Talia, but remembering her clan somehow made their absence a little more bearable.

One evening, as Caitlin laid out a simple meal of apples, gruel and aged cheese, she realized with a start that the dusky colours of the day had lulled and the sky outside had darkened. Joshua was late for supper. Where was that boy? Probably somewhere nearby moping for home again. But he was never late. Could something have happened?

The dire tones of the prophecy were back in Caitlin's thoughts. She started shaking as terror gave wings to her feet. She ran outside, her worry for Joshua blinding her, and ran straight into the arms of a stranger. He was a short, ugly man, and behind him, slightly to his right, stood a thin, taller and academic looking man who seemed quite out of place in the wilds of Szevaci. The short and squat man gripped her arms. His coarse hand roughly caressed her head in manner that nearly made her sick while his other hand remained clasped tightly around her waist. She couldn't escape. Hopefully these two men were merely random thugs looking for food, shelter or coin and would soon be gone once they realized her little cottage hid no riches. Her senses were screaming danger but she tried desperately to keep calm. She couldn't see Joshua with them. She hoped that he would continue to linger by the river and the men wouldn't see him at all.

"Is she one of them?" her captor asked the second man in a guttural voice.

Caitlin felt the panic welling up inside her on hearing these words. She only had to see the fanatic look creeping into the eyes of the thin man as he gaped at her blue hair to know the truth. She saw knowledge and recognition of its true origins and she felt afraid.

Caitlin was about to ask what they wanted from her when, as though waking up from a stupor, the second man screeched at her captor. "Garcia, shut her mouth so she won't be able to cast a spell on us and turn us into frogs or something!"

As Garcia's rough hand shifted from her hair to her mouth, almost cutting of her air in the process, Caitlin felt her hopes sinking. They were here for her. It was no coincidence. They knew she was a sorceress. She tried to escape by struggling and kicking out her legs, but the man shook her like a rag doll.

Her thoughts turned to Joshua. She hoped that they would not find him. She hoped Joshua would somehow escape and find his way back to his father and sister. But Aberevon was so far away.

Caitlin struggled even more frantically. She had to get away and save Joshua. If only her medallion were with her right now. She couldn't use magic to save herself, not with her mouth covered and her hands trapped in that horrible man's grip. She should have reacted faster. She started wriggling again, wearing out her captor's patience. He gave an angry grunt. Her vision blurred and her legs crumpled beneath her with the vicious blow he struck on her head. She collapsed with a shrill ringing resounding in her ears. Then there was only a restless darkness.

Before they bundled Caitlin up for the journey back to Aberevon, the enterprising historian forced a mixture concocted from lemon balm leaves and the flowers of the valerian hop plants down her throat to ensure she would sleep the rest of the journey. Neither man wanted the witch to try some magic on them before they were ready for her. The potion quickly took effect. Caitlin did not move; she did not moan. She was utterly still, her face pale and drawn. She could have easily been mistaken for dead.

Joshua burst in on the two men just as Garcia hoisted Caitlin onto his shoulder. Joshua was a Heichi beyond doubt. He did not have magic, but all Heichi sons had brave hearts. They lacked immortality and power but not courage and valour. Joshua was no exception. He had always seen himself as Talia's knight, and now he was his mother's. It didn't occur to him that he was only seven years old. For Joshua, a son was bound by a code of honour to his mother.

He was a knight without a dragon or a horse but he wouldn't turn his tail and run.

Joshua took in the scene before him, his little body twitching with raw anger pumping unusual strength into his limbs allowing him to push Garcia to the ground. The surprised hunter fell, taking Caitlin with him. Garcia's eyes blazed with acrimony, but Joshua saw none of it. He only saw Caitlin's tightly closed eyes. "What have you done to my mama?" he yelled, rage and fear searing his childish voice. Then, as though unable to contain the violent emotions bursting within, he started pummelling Garcia with his tiny fists.

"Do something, you fool!" Garcia yelled at the gaping Luigi. "What are you waiting for? Grab him!" Garcia found himself partly trapped under Caitlin's still body and unable to handle the boy.

The historian had indeed been standing motionless observing the goings-on with an air of astonishment. He was a true academician in both body and soul. He was a believer of science and logic, yet his greatest achievement was discovering the ancient text alluding to the Heichi sorceresses. To learn that there were sorceresses belonging to a secret clan and the possibility that some still dwelled on Earth excited him tremendously. The king needed a sorceress, just one of them, and they had found her. But reality and theories extolled in books are two entirely different matters. The historian learned this the hard way.

Luigi often found himself cowing before Garcia during their travels. The man had a temper and unbelievable strength. What punishment would the hunter inflict for Luigi's ineptness in dealing with a mere child? To see a little boy confront the king's most powerful hunter so bravely left Luigi stunned and rooted to the spot. He knew Garcia would be greatly disappointed in him. But try as he might, Luigi couldn't bring himself to harm or even restrain the boy. At the back of his mind, he knew Garcia would exact his revenge. He managed to feel a slight twinge of pity for the boy rather than himself. If not today, then tomorrow, or months from now, but Garcia would kill the boy. Nothing less would satisfy him. He was known for his vengeful nature.

Garcia managed to extract himself from under Caitlin's still body without any assistance from Luigi at all. Ignoring the gaping man, he grabbed the boy. He forced the sleeping potion down the child's throat instead of throttling him like he wanted to. Maybe he should strangle Luigi instead for his ineffectual assistance. It would at least soothe his wounded ego.

CHAPTER XII

I saw the power Damien had over you. I know your actions were governed by your love for Joshua. In all his innocence and purity, Joshua became a weapon that Damien used against you.

You fought tooth and nail against the prophecy of the Wraith, but it in the end, your every thought and action only took you closer to its fulfilment. Was this destiny?

Talia

BROKEN—CAITLIN

CAITLIN STOOD BEFORE KING DAMIEN. She looked proud and determined but her mind was filled with questions and worries. She was back in Aberevon, her home, but as a captive. After all her efforts to put distance between herself and Talia, she was right back where she started. Michael and Talia were so near yet so far.

Did the king know about her kinship with them? The king's hunters had found her far north, which she hoped meant the king did not know about Talia.

Caitlin hadn't seen any sign of Joshua since she regained consciousness, nor had anyone mentioned him. Did this mean he'd managed to escape? Could she dare hope?

Caitlin stared straight ahead, but the words of her old friend Ava swirled through her mind, weakening her knees with fear. *Always remember that you are in possession of a unique gift. Everlasting youth, an elixir humans are constantly in search of. You must protect your secret at all costs.* How much did Damien know about her? She remembered all the rumours she had heard about him, his brutal and cunning nature, and that he'd killed his own father for the throne. Michael had always sheltered her and the children from the king and his henchmen, but now she stood before him, alone and vulnerable.

As if reading her mind, Damien asked, "Do you know of my friend Ava? You look just like her. Are you one of her sisters?" Caitlin didn't say a word. However hard she tried to mask her surprise, it showed in her eyes; she couldn't help it. Was he a magical being too? How could he know that she was thinking of Ava? How did he know Ava at all? He wasn't supposed to know of sorceresses.

"Ah," the king said, rubbing his hands in delight. "I was almost beginning to think I'd imagined her." Grinning, he asked, "So tell me this. Why were you hiding in a remote corner of the world where there are neither supernaturals nor humans? Don't you have any other family? Did you know I was looking for you?"

The king saw the fear in her eyes. He smiled to himself. *So she does have family other than the boy.* He would give her time and then reel her into his trap. For now, the boy would suffice to make her do his bidding, and then he would uncover the remaining members of her family. Hopefully there was another sorceress or two hidden somewhere. He wanted all the power he could get.

The king commanded a private meeting with Caitlin, but only after ensuring she was well bound so she could do no magic. He asked for all his men to leave the room. He could see her confusion. She could not understand what was happening.

"Let me introduce myself properly," he said. "I am Damien, King of Aberevon."

"I already know that," she muttered, realizing her mistake. He must not realize she was from Aberevon. It would lead him to Michael and Talia.

Luckily, caught up in his own speech, Damien did not hear her. He was saying, "I am the king of Aberevon, but this is not my time. Your friend Ava brought me here from the past." He whispered into her ear even though they were alone, "She made me journey through time when I was just a boy, and because of that, I am dying slowly each day, and no one *here* seems to be able to be able cure me."

"Everyone dies," Caitlin said sharply. "Accept it."

"But not *you*, not Ava. Why? What is so special about you?" the king shouted. "I am the chosen one. I am king. This is my destiny. There is much for me to do. My time is not done. I will not die because *you* will save me. Do you take me for a fool? Why do you think I brought you here?" he asked dramatically. "I know your secret. You are an immortal sorceress. Either tell me where to find Ava, or use your magic to make me whole again."

Caitlin shook her head vehemently. She didn't know Ava's whereabouts. She hadn't seen her friend in years. She couldn't tell him about Nabia and the medallion because he would kill all the children. *I didn't ask for immortality. All I wanted was a family. Why has this mad man brought me here, she who has washed her hands of her supernatural ancestry? How does he know so much?*

King Damien smirked as he saw her panic and denial. "Ava isn't here. You are. You will do. You have to cure me and make me immortal like you."

Caitlin stared at him in shock. "You ask for the impossible," she said. "I don't know how to do what you ask. I gave up magic a long time ago. I can't help you. I can't."

"I promised," she added softy, almost to herself.

King Damien laughed. "You can't or you won't? Promises are meant to be broken; don't you know that?" he sang out in a singsong voice. But he saw the grim twist of her mouth. She was going to be difficult. A steadfast and unflinching look crept into her expression and in the way she squared her shoulders and looked him in the eye. She had taken on an air of a detachment. She seemed to be saying to him: *Do your worst but I will not give you what you need.*

Well, he was about to prove her wrong. She would soon be falling over herself to please him. He was about to give her an incentive.

He clapped his hands. The time for games was over. It was time for him to take control. "Bring him," he shouted. At his command, a small door at the bottom of the steps leading down from the throne swung open. A tall, brutal looking soldier entered. Frozen and paralyzed, Caitlin had eyes only for her seven-year-old son.

"Mama!" Joshua shouted on seeing her. Wriggling out of the soldier's grip, he ran to Caitlin, his little arms holding on tight. "Mama, Mama," was all he could say. Caitlin felt the words stick in her throat. She kissed his head and mumbled, "It will be all right." She knew she was lying. The stakes had changed. Everything was different now that King Damien had Joshua in his clutches. He had been toying with her all along.

"You will do what I ask," the evil king said, oblivious to her self-recriminations. "Or he will suffer each time you refuse." Caitlin fell to her knees wailing in terror, begging for her son's life to be spared. She had no pride or self respect anymore. All thoughts of honouring her Heichi sisterhood were wiped from her head. At this moment, she was just a mother desperate to save her child. "I will do as you say." The wheels of the prophecy were truly turning. Soon Caitlin would be on the path of no return.

THE HEICHI never used their powers except for the good of others, so working against her inherent nature took a tremendous toll on Caitlin. As she worked her magic, Damien's weakness fell away, cast from his body like a snake shedding its old skin. The stronger he became, the weaker she grew. Her youth was fading fast. It was as if he was absorbing her vitality and her power, saving nothing for her. Damien forced Caitlin to break every tenet the Heichi held dear, including summoning a magical creature from Htrae, a powerful dragon he imprisoned in his dungeon.

If this continued, immortal or not, Caitlin would soon be nothing but an empty shell.

Caitlin's fading strength and youth did not matter to her in the least. Going against the vow she had made all that time ago tore at her, but every time she hesitated, Joshua suffered. Damien had a whip that he casually slashed against the little boy's torso as if he were but a doll made of stone. But Joshua was only human, a boy made of skin and bones, and so his screams of pain would tear at Caitlin's heart, bringing her conformity even before the next lash fell.

Joshua knew he had become his mother's weakness. Every time the lash flew, the little boy couldn't help but cry out in pain however hard he tried to hold back the screams. He was scared, badly bruised and terrified, but he bore the anguish with as much grace and fortitude as he could for his mother's sake.

More than his own torture, it was the harsh treatment being meted out to his mother that affected the already weakened child and upset him. Ever day he saw the light in her eyes grow dimmer. It was always Garcia who took special pleasure in tormenting Caitlin because he knew it riled the boy. Nobody but the king could lay hands on the boy, but no one said anything about Caitlin being off limits.

Ever since Joshua had attacked Garcia and enjoyed the upper hand for a brief moment, the hunter bore an unreasonable grouse against him. Luigi had been right; Garcia was after vengeance.

The breaking point came when, one day, Garcia took a knife to Caitlin's delicate skin, cutting her arms in random motions as though it was all nothing but a game to him. Joshua, as expected, went mad with rage. The little boy elbowed one soldier, knocking him to the ground. He kicked another on the shin and tried to make his way to Caitlin.

"Stay, stay," Caitlin pleaded with him, but it was too late. The fallen soldier's hands moved, and without any thought of the consequences, he threw a spear at the running boy.

"No! No!" Caitlin raged in protest, but it was too late. Garcia stared open mouthed at the fallen child. He hadn't intended for him to die. He needed to put as much distance between himself and the boy as possible, otherwise King Damien would have his head. In the interest of self-preservation, Garcia quickly fled the dungeon.

A bleeding Joshua somehow made it to a chained Caitlin. Her screams had stopped. All that emerged were stifled sobs as Joshua lay at her feet barely breathing. Even at the end, he was so full of love. "I love you, Mama. Tell Talia…" he began to say, but then a trickle of blood gurgled from his mouth and he closed his eyes.

Caitlin felt herself go over the edge. She no longer had any reason to be submissive. She lost all her restraint and timidity.

In that moment, at the point of losing Joshua, she saw the truth. A mother always feels the most protective towards the weakest of her flock. She loved her fragile, innocent and wonderful son more much more than she even loved her husband or daughter because his vulnerability made him all the more cherished. She couldn't exist after what had been done to him. If it were possible to will her own life force to fade away, she would have done so.

CHAPTER XIII

It was just a few fleeting moments. Joshua and you spent two years in the custody of that villain, Damien. After that, my life as I knew it was over. The terror he inspired in Father and I put wings to my feet and took me far away, as it did my peace of mind.

Talia

𝒟AMIEN FINDS HIS QUEEN—TALIA

BY THE TIME Damien heard of the chaos in the dungeon, it was all over. He only caught sight of several pale apparitions, translucent like wisps of mist surrounding Caitlin, and then there was nothing. *Ghosts*, he thought, crossing himself to ward them off, although they showed not the slightest interest in him. Their entire attention was centred on Caitlin and the body of her son in her arms.

He wanted to know what had happened and how his guards

had lost control of the situation. Things had been going so well. He had been growing stronger and healthier each day. He caught a glimpse of the bodies of his soldiers lying lifeless on the stone floor and a rage crept through him. Those bumbling idiots must have messed up. Some action of theirs had summoned the magical beings into their midst, he was sure of it. Garcia, who was nowhere in sight, would hopefully have some inkling of what had transpired in the dungeon.

A week later, as Damien took stock, he realized the situation was not entirely hopeless. Caitlin had been in his custody for almost two years; her boy wouldn't have lasted much longer, and Damien knew that with his death, his hold on Caitlin would end. That is why he had already initiated the search for the rest of her family. Luigi and Garcia had worked well in finding Caitlin, so there was no reason the same duo couldn't replicate their *magic*, so to speak, again.

Garcia had a soul driven by greed, so a bag full of gold coins would galvanize him into action. But what of Luigi? Reluctance streamed from every pore. Only the thought of saving himself and his brother had motivated him the last time around. Damien's spies had informed him that Luigi's stoic and reticent elder brother had just returned from a failed trip to Zedresh. He hadn't managed to find a sorceress, which gave Damien a reason to throw Marco in prison.

If Luigi wanted his brother freed, he would have to find Caitlin's family for Damien. They, in turn, would help him find another sorceress. The situation was still very much retrievable and Damien had a good feeling. His luck had not yet turned. Caitlin's magic had been invaluable to him. Despite the absence of a sorceress, all was not lost for he still had the dragon she had summoned for him. His very own magnificent dragon chained and imprisoned in the dungeon. His to command and use as he pleased. No one would be able to stop him from world domination now.

~

AT DAMIEN'S COMMAND, Marco was thrown into a cell. To earn his brother's freedom, Luigi was tasked with finding the rest of Caitlin's family. The weary historian prepared to travel north with Garcia back to Szevaci to find Caitlin's family. The excitement of the search had left Luigi but he would do anything to save his older brother. Before leaving, he went to visit Marco.

"Do not worry, Marco. I will get you out of here," Luigi told him.

"At what cost?" his brother said. "By throwing more people into this prison instead of me? Is that fair? Don't we have a god to answer to someday? I would rather you leave me to rot here and take this chance to run away and never return to this awful place."

"How can I abandon you?" Luigi asked. "You are my family."

"I don't want you to do something horrible just to save me. I am sure the king will ask you to commit a crime in return for saving me. During the search for the elusive sorceress, the king needlessly slaughtered our innocent friends just because we didn't believe *she* existed. I tell you he is mad."

Luigi sighed. Marco didn't know that truth. He didn't know that Luigi had been the one to find the sorceress. Hearing Marco's next words, Luigi was glad he had held his tongue.

"What kind of a man throws a child into the dungeon? A little boy was imprisoned in the next cell," Marco said, unaware of the fate that had befallen Joshua. "He was tortured and now I am even more fearful for him because he seems to have been moved to another location. There is no sign of him or his mother now. I curse the vile man who brought the boy to the king. I am sure it was one of the evil hunters. Just as you are my family, the little boy in the next cell next has family. He used to always talk about his sister in his sleep. It is a pity that even though she is in Aberevon itself, she didn't know that her brother was here."

Luigi, who had barely being paying attention to Marco's

ramblings, snapped to attention at the mention of Joshua's name. "What did you say?" asked Luigi, almost sure he had heard wrong.

"I am touched to see your concern for my little friend but his story won't help us in any way. The only thing it tells me is that you must flee and never return," said Marco. "I don't want you to die too."

"No. Not that. What did you say about the *boy's family?*" said Luigi, his irritation showing.

"How does it matter to you?" asked a hurt Marco. "Unless you intend to help them," he said, hope burning in his eyes.

"Yes, yes I do!" exclaimed Luigi, hoping that Marco wouldn't see the deceit in his eyes.

"Oh! Then this changes things," said a relieved Marco. "The boy, Joshua, has family in Aberevon. His father is a merchant, Michael, and he has an older sister called Talia. The mother—"

"I don't need to know about the mother," Luigi interrupted. She was gone; Caitlin's story didn't matter anymore. From what he had pieced together, her tale was quite tragic; he didn't want his conscience raising its head at the wrong moment. He had to focus on saving his brother.

Luigi almost ran to the king immediately. "Anything else you remember, brother?" he asked with barely restrained patience. "Don't worry; you will be out of here in no time."

"Nothing more," said a puzzled Marco, unable to fully compre-hend his brother's motives and connection between his own freedom and Joshua's family.

As Luigi gave Marco a cursory hug and prepared to leave, he wasn't prepared for the rawness in Marco's eyes. His soul protested at his determination to lie to his own brother.

"But why are you so interested in them? Will you help reunite him with his family?" Marco asked before Luigi left. In his brother's hesitation, Marco saw the truth and realized he had been duped. Luigi was willing to do anything, right or wrong, to save his brother. *This isn't right*, thought Marco. *I need to remove myself from this situation so that my brother is forced to do the right thing.*

And that is exactly what he did a few days later.

∾

BARELY A WEEK after the incident in the dungeon, a spy returned with news. The family had been found and, wonder of wonders, there was a daughter. *Another sorceress—Caitlin's replacement.* Talia sounded perfect. It was time to meet her, to bring her in. Damien had to be careful this time. She was his last hope. He could not lose her too. He would handle this himself and keep his violent and stupid men out of it.

Late one evening, Damien followed Talia while she was out; she was accompanied only by a single maid. As he watched her from his carriage, he was won over by her self-assurance.

Talia was slender in a way that implied she had suddenly lost weight. She had the air of a person who carried a deep sorrow within them. Despite that, there was a poise with which she held herself, which reminded Damien of a gently curling wave as it moved away from the seashore. Her face held so much character, nothing like the glorious but vapid beauties of his court. It was flawless except for the wrinkle between her eyes as she frowned in concentration.

Other than her face, Talia was covered from head to toe. Damien couldn't see her hair, but he knew it would be blue like her mother's. Her preoccupied eyes shone bright with either the brilliance of unshed tears or the glimmer of hope; he couldn't make out which. Maybe he already knew enough about her life, but the fact was, this was a face that had seen a lot of pain but still retained innocence and kindness. Something he had never known.

Beauty, vulnerability, and power; an enticing combination attracting Damien to Talia. He couldn't wait to meet her. She was

83

little more than a child but she had to belong to him. She would be both his queen and his enchantress.

As he watched, a sudden gust of wind blew Talia's empty basket away. Dodging the passing carriages, she gave it chase. Hard as she held on to her hood, it still fluttered in the breeze. Her mother had always warned her of the locals' dislike for the blue hair that ran in their family. Since childhood, Talia had been instructed to hide her hair in the presence of others. Engrossed in play, she had accepted her mother's words without questioning them and had diligently followed them all these years.

As her basket danced along the path driven by the whims of the wind, the king watched her coming closer and closer. She was indeed exquisite. It was her destiny to be his and she was coming to him of her own accord.

When Damien could no longer control his eagerness to speak to Talia, he stepped out of his carriage. She had finally caught up with the errant basket and was standing right in front of the royal carriage, a sheepish smile on her face.

Sensing movement, Talia quickly looked up. Seeing Damien, her smile faded and her face took on a hunted expression. She obviously recognized him; he had to do something about that nasty reputation of his. As the king stared at her, unable to keep the yearning from his eyes, her expression turned even more wary. He could see how her eyes had taken on the look of a hunted deer. It was only out of her ingrained politeness she clumsily tried to curtsy, but he knew that she would rather flee.

It was time to begin a conversation and win her over. "You are Caitlin's daughter," he said. A statement, not a question. It was best to use the element of surprise. "Your mother will be so glad I found you," said the king in his usual grandiose manner.

Hearing the word *mother*, the girl was disarmed. "My mother? You've found her? Is my brother with her too? Are they coming home?" she asked, her words tumbling over each other in her eagerness to get them out. Damien saw her hope overcome her misgivings about him. In her great hurry to learn the whereabouts of her mother and brother, she did not even ask how he knew who she was. His sorceress was so precious and innocent and so pathetically eager to meet her family. If he were capable of it, King Damien would actually feel sorry for her.

Talia begged to know about their welfare. "Are they all right?" she asked.

He told lie after lie. Her mother came to him with a problem. Someone was chasing her and she was afraid for her life. She had sought his protection.

"Why didn't she tell father?" Talia wondered aloud.

"Because she was afraid you and your father would have been harmed too." Damien was having fun. The lies were coming to him so easily he almost believed them himself. Telling the truth wasn't going to win her over; besides, it was such a pleasure to see her face light up he could not disappoint her now. She had to continue believing Caitlin and her brother were alive and well.

"If you come with me, everything will be all right (for me, that is). Your mother will be so glad to see you. I can tell you more on the way," he said, forcing a sincere and mild tone into his voice.

Talia was about to enter the carriage when she recalled the words her mother had drilled into her a long, long time ago when they used to train together. Never trust someone you've just met. Give yourself time to understand their motives however sincere they may seem.

Talia stopped. She had been about to act so hastily. She knew she needed her father's counsel. She spoke up quickly. "I know where the palace is. I will be there tomorrow with my father."

He had waited so long. What was another day? "Very well," he muttered, feeling romantic and generous. After all, she was to be his queen. He had to grant at least a few of her wishes as she was going to fulfil so many of his. "Make sure I see you there," were his last words to her.

Damien spent the night building plans. He would treat Talia

with love, and she would give him a new lease on life just like her mother had. They would be terribly happy and he would rule the world with her by his side.

Unfortunately for Damien, his dream remained just that. Talia did not show up at the palace the followng morning. He sent soldiers in search of her but they returned empty handed. It seemed that she had fled Aberevon. She had played him for a fool.

It was time to dispatch his hunters to search for Talia. The message was clear. *Don't return until you have found her.* The hunters travelled to far-flung areas while the soldiers continued to look locally. Anyone who returned empty handed would be put to death, so they devised a devious way of diverting the king's wrath. They would present any girl whose hair had the slightest glint of blue—innocent daughters, wives and sisters—to the king.

Initially, their apparent incompetence annoyed the king. Then he began to enjoy it. This was a game of the hunter and the hunted. Each girl had to prove her immortality against the executioner's sword. Only if she survived would he take her as his bride. But no human can endure against a sword passing through their middle.

The king would have loved to have sacrificed the girls to his dragon. He basked in the mayhem him and his dragon forged together. To him, the dragon was a facilitator of terror. The dragon was an unexpected gift, but ever since Caitlin had disappeared with those ghosts, the wretched creature had changed. Spewing flames while flying in the sky and causing havoc all around was something the dragon could be forced into, but taking the life of a person standing in front of him was something the creature refused to do.

When the first girl was pushed into the dragon's chamber, her screams were heard far and wide. Damien was pleased, but in the end, it turned out she was hale and hearty. She had only shrieked and screamed because the lonely dragon had tried to befriend her, forgetting how scary he would seem to her.

Damien had killed her himself. No more dragon sacrifices after that.

Countless innocents died but Damien felt no guilt. It was all Talia's fault for running away. Death became a game of distraction from what was happening to his insides. He could feel himself getting sicker each day. Talia had to be found, and soon.

CHAPTER XIV

My father always told me that nobody is infallible. He warned me that everyone has a breaking point. He knew I was a Heichi sorceress even if I did not know my own legacy. As a father, he wanted me to be capable of protecting myself in the future, and he wanted me to overcome my vulnerabilities.

But the thing about chinks in our armour is that they are mostly bound to and interwoven with the ones we love. We can't know what will break us until it happens.

Losing you, Mother, broke Father because you were the love of his life.

Talia

A DAUGHTER'S PROMISE—TALIA

MICHAEL COULDN'T BELIEVE it was almost four years since Caitlin and Joshua had gone missing. The years had been a blur of disappointments, false hopes and clutching at straws. He had announced large rewards for news of a woman and a young boy. There were many sightings but by the time Michael would arrive, either the trail had run cold or the lead turned out to be a false one.

His Jaesdan friends noticed his absence. The boys and Nabia visited once. Nabia hadn't been able to meet his eyes.

Joshua was five to Talia's twelve when Caitlin and him disappeared. If Joshua were still alive, he would now be almost nine. Michael's life had revolved around his wife and his children. Without them, there was an empty space in his heart, which ached constantly.

For a long time, Michael trusted that Caitlin would return with Joshua. When she didn't, he was optimistic about finding them himself. As each day passed with no trace of his lost family, a little part of him began to wither and die.

Michael found himself slipping away from Talia. He knew it wasn't fair to her. She needed her father. He had to try harder. The child worked tirelessly to maintain the façade of a normal household and to give him a sense of normality despite all they had been through. But every time he tried to smile, a memory of Caitlin crept up on him and he found himself melancholy again.

Sometimes Talia's brave façade slipped a little and Michael would get a glimpse of her grief, but then the mask would be firmly back in place.

One day when Talia was out, Michael had a visitor.

Michael was apologetic. "Are you a merchant too? I am sorry but I no longer trade. If you have any goods to sell, I cannot take them on for you."

"No, sir, I am not a trader. I work for the king. You must listen to me. My name is Luigi and I have come to warn you that your daughter is in grave danger."

"Whatever do you mean?" asked a scared Michael.

"Please believe what I tell you. You have a very short window to save your daughter, otherwise she will be gone forever just like your wife and son."

Michael felt the breath whoosh out of him, as though someone had punched him in the stomach. "My wife and son? What do you know about their disappearance? Where are they? What has happened to them?"

"I am truly sorry," said Luigi

"What do you mean?" asked Michael, a cold dread circling his heart. But he already knew what the man was going to tell him. He was going to confirm the fear that kept Michael awake at night, his worst nightmare, the death of his wife and son.

Although his expression said it all, Luigi knew the importance of saying it loud and clear, otherwise a grief-stricken family could live each day on tenterhooks with the possibility or hope of good news. Luigi needed Michael to be alert, for a storm in the form of Damien would soon be coming his way. He had to know the truth.

"They are dead. Both gone," said Luigi. Michael almost fell, but Luigi supported him and continued urgently. "I am not sure if you are aware but your wife was a sorceress. The king wanted her power. By threatening to hurt your son, he made her do his bidding. But a few days back, something went wrong and they both died."

Michael mourned for Caitlin and Joshua. Were his wife and son gone forever? Michael shook his head. Joshua could be killed, but not Caitlin. She still lived; he was sure of it. She had told him of her immortality.

"She can't die. She is...." Michael stopped, still reluctant to divulge Caitlin's long held secret.

"Immortal?" Luigi finished for him. "Maybe once but not anymore. King Damien took all of her power. She was very weak towards the end."

"Why should I believe any of this?" a heartbroken Michael exclaimed. "Why should I mourn my family on the words of a stranger?"

"For one reason only. Your daughter needs you," said Luigi "The king forced your wife use her power to heal him. Something went wrong in the dungeon where she and your son were being held," said Luigi, breaking down. "No one really saw what happened, maybe only the king, but whatever he saw convinced him that your wife was gone forever, which is the reason he became even more desperate in his search for what remains of your family."

"Why?" asked a heartbroken Michael. "Hasn't he taken enough?"

"For Damien, until he possesses you or has broken you, body and soul, there is no such thing as enough," said Luigi matter of factly. Michael could sense Luigi's pain despite his own towering anguish.

"The king thinks your daughter is a sorceress like her mother," Luigi continued softly.

This man is scaring me, thought Michael. *He seems to know my worst fears.* "Does the king already have Talia?" asked Michael, his breath in abeyance waiting for Luigi's answer. "Is that the bad news you are hiding from me?"

"Not that I know of. But he will soon have her if we don't act quickly. Where is your daughter?"

"She is out running some errands. She should be fine. She knows how to look after herself," said Michael, although worry gnawed at him.

"I pray for her safe return. The king mustn't find her tonight," said Luigi. "He won't harm her; he wants to marry her. He wants her for her power. He already knows everything about the both of you. I am the one who told him about you. I told him in the hope that he would release my brother, Marco. Marco was a much better man than me. A good man. He was in prison with your son. He would comfort the boy in the dark dungeons. When he learned your son was dead and that I was the man responsible for kidnapping him and your wife, he killed himself." Luigi started sobbing. Michael bowed his head in pain. "He was my only brother and he put an end to his own life to force me to do the right thing. He was extremely fond of your son. His last wish was for your son's family to be shielded from further harm. So here I am to honour his wish."

"I am very thankful to your brother and you. May the lord bless his departed soul," said Michael, recognising the man's pain.

"Are you one of his famed hunters?" Michael asked, trying to get the measure of the man in front of him.

"No, not at all. I am not a spy or a fighter. I am merely a historian. I also helped…" He couldn't go on.

"You helped with what?" asked Michael.

"I am the scum, the hellhound who helped kidnap your wife and son. You can kill me, sir; I will not utter a word of protest."

Michael was silent for a long time. Grief tore at his soul. He wanted to lock himself up in a room and never emerge again. Ever since Caitlin and Joshua were lost to him, he hadn't been a very good father. He had to put Talia first now. She was all he had.

If Luigi could save Talia, Michael would be beholden to him all his life.

"What will killing you get me? Will it bring Caitlin and Joshua back? Did you mean what you said about saving my daughter?" Luigi nodded. "But how can she escape?" asked a distraught Michael, vacillating between despair and hope. His head was beginning to spin and he couldn't think straight anymore. "If the king knows, there is no place we can hide."

"You must both leave Aberevon. I have arranged passage on a ship sailing out of Aberevon. It is not going far; just a few ports down, but it will be a start. It will be enough to throw the search effort into disarray. Thereafter, you can decide where you want to go. The less I know, the safer you are. Here is the name of the ship and the captain. He is my wife's cousin and can be trusted." Luigi pressed the information into the hands of a dazed Michael.

"Thank you," said Michael. This man may have done irreparable harm to his family, but he was also trying to make amends. He had risked a lot by coming to warn him.

"Luigi clasped Michael's hand and then he was gone.

WHEN TALIA RUSHED HOME DISTRESSED by her unorthodox exchange with King Damien, her father knew at once that the king had found her. *Thank God he didn't snatch her.* On hearing her out, Michael realized just how narrow her escape had been. He had to get her out of Aberevon. He knew they didn't have much time.

Michael's hands started shaking as the enormity of the decision he faced struck him. Luigi wanted to save them both, but if everything went according to plan, he could never see his daughter again, for he had no intention of leaving with Talia. Both he and Caitlin had prepared her for this very day when she would have to protect herself. Michael had to stay to find out what happened to Caitlin and Joshua, but Talia must leave and live her life freely, not in the shadow of a monster. Only sixteen years old and she had already seen too much of the harsh realities of life. Talia deserved some happiness.

It had taken a crisis for Michael to finally wake up and see how much his daughter needed him. Now that he had, there was no way he would let her down. He would get her away from Aberevon with Luigi's help, and then her training would kick in. He had seen Talia in action. He knew just how strong his little girl was, both on the outside and in.

Caitlin and Joshua were lost for eternity. He would mourn for

them later. The challenge was to break the news to Talia. She had
to know the truth. If he didn't tell her, she wouldn't take him seri-
ously and would refuse to leave.

Michael told Talia his plan. "I am taking you to the harbour.
You must leave Aberevon immediately," he said.

Talia was shocked. Disobeying the king was an offence punish-
able by death.

"You are in grave danger from the king himself," Michael said
urgently. There was no way to soften the blow. "He has probably
killed your mother and brother. I can't lose you too."

The fear of losing Talia was so great it felt like a huge fist
squeezing his heart. There was no time to be lost but he knew
how stubborn Talia could be. When it came to family, she was just
like him. She wouldn't budge without an explanation. How right
he was.

Talia's face had already taken on an adamant expression. She
was going to dig her heels in. It would be too late if he didn't act
now. "Father, I don't understand; the king told me he has them.
Why would he lie?" she said in despair. Her father had to
be wrong.

"I promise to tell you if, in return, you promise to leave
Aberevon. Never will you turn back. No matter what," Michael
conceded.

"What kind of a promise is that?" grumbled Talia. "It doesn't
sound fair."

"I am the father here. It is my right to decide," Michael stated.
Talia must not trust King Damien's foul lies at any cost. A harsh
reality that would protect her was better than the king's
wonderfully spun tales of hope that would put her in
harm's way.

With Michael's unvarnished plain speaking, Talia's life
changed forever. "It is a trap. He does not have them," he said.
"What King Damien claims could never happen. Your mother
would never seek shelter with such a man. He is not one to help

people out of the goodness of his heart. Open your eyes," he pleaded.

"To what?" Talia whispered.

"Your mother would never have left if she intended to come back. You and I have suspected this for some time but we have been in denial. We must accept it now. Your safety hinges on this. I have been told that King Damien killed her and...Jo...Joshua too." Michael's voice cracked. It was a while before he could continue as Talia stood shaking with grief.

"How do you know it is true?" she asked.

"I just do. There are things about her life and your own that you do not know, but it seems that King Damien does, as did my informant. He would not have been lying. He didn't need to."

There was no sound for a long time except for Talia's woeful sobs. "So now what?" she finally asked.

"You leave."

Talia walked to the window in a trance. Her father was right. The king must have been lying about them being alive. There had been a fake and cheery ring to his entire demeanour. But he must have had her mother and Joshua at some point. She felt sure of this.

In the distance, she could see the lone tower of the palace rising up towards the sky, soaring above the surrounding trees in the vicinity. Had King Damien held them there? Or was it in his famous dark dungeon where many a prisoner was rumoured to have been discarded and forgotten about? Could it be possible that they had been so very close yet out of reach all this while? There were no more tears to be shed. They had to be avenged. She turned to her father.

"Why me? Why does he want me?" Talia finally asked the all important, defining question.

"You may not like what you hear," he said. Her father's words puzzled her, but her head was already reeling, so she remained silent waiting for his reply. He had just alluded that her loving mother and her precious little brother were dead. What could be worse than that? She had nothing more to lose except him.

Michael held nothing back. He told her the whole truth about her ancestry, why Caitlin had abandoned the Heichi, and how powerful Talia could be if she knew the secrets of her Heichi heritage. Talia realized that she was neither fully human nor a sorceress. *What was she?*

"You are our daughter; that is what you are. We have loved you, cherished you and taught you everything we know. You may not know how to use magic but it lies within you. I saw your mother use magic only once. It was to save my life, and she was wonderful. You want revenge but you are not ready to deal with the likes of King Damien. You are worn out with sorrow, confusion and the stress of the past four years. Besides, you are only sixteen. Face him now and I will lose another person I love."

"Is there really magic in this world?" she asked. "I find it difficult to believe."

"I think there is magic in your soul and your heart. All you need to do is look inside and you will find it. Not today, maybe, but someday." Michael fell silent for a while and then continued. "Your mother told me that that your powers manifested mostly when you were angry. Do you ever recall unexplained things happening around you?"

Talia gasped. She realized what her father meant. "I hurt mother sometimes without meaning to while we trained together. I remember I would get frustrated because I couldn't seem to get the better of her, or I would want to stop but she would insist on practising. At those times, it would suddenly seem that an invisible force threw her away from me."

Michael smiled sadly. "Yes, Talia, I know. Your mother told me you had started using magic without even being aware of it. She thought that maybe, as a half blood, your magic was innate compared to how it was for her. She was so proud of you."

"How could she be proud? I hurt her. I hurt her, Father, but I didn't mean to. You know that." Talia was tearful.

"I do. And so did she. As if you are capable of hurting anyone, least of all someone you love. It only means that while you are as magical as your mother, if not more so, you are also different," Michael told her. "But you mustn't worry about harming someone inadvertently because your mother was never badly hurt by your actions. I am sure that as you grow older, your control will improve."

"I wish she had taught me how to use and control my powers," said Talia wistfully.

"Your mother had her reasons. I believe one of them was to protect our family. The family she came from wouldn't approve of me in her life. After our marriage, she hid her supernatural nature to keep her identity secret. She turned her back on her sisters, others just like her," he said, regret lacing his voice. "Your brother and you were the most magical things in our lives."

"Was Joshua magical too?" asked Talia suddenly, trying to disguise the hope in her voice.

"No, Talia," said Michael flatly. "If you are asking because you think their magic would have saved them, you are wrong."

"Why?" Talia asked, tears clouding her eyes.

"Only daughters inherit the power of their mothers. Your mother told me that magic would be harmful to Joshua."

"Please don't say that, Father," pleaded Talia.

"Your time will come. Your power is still in its nascent stage. You are still young. You must hide until you are older," Michael cautioned.

"Will you be coming with me?" Talia asked. Seeing Michael's expression, she understood the truth. "You want me to run away alone. Why?" Talia was crying now.

Michael hesitated but then he confessed, "I must stay here. I owe it to your mother and brother. I have to learn what happened to them."

"What kind of position are you putting me in? I can't avenge them. I can't look for them. I have to run and hide like a coward while you get to stay behind and become a martyr. Why? Because you are the father and husband? Am I not a sister and a daughter? Don't I get a say in this? Don't make me leave you, Father. I can help. I must help."

But Michael shook his head. He wanted to hold Talia in his arms and weep, but he had to remember the danger. "Don't be silly, girl. I am not going to do anything foolish, but I promised your mother I would never leave her. I also promised her I would always look out for you. Let me keep my word. You, in turn, remember your promise to me. It is not safe for you here, but I have nothing to fear. The man who warned me may help me hide from the king. You must go and begin a new life alone. Together we will be much too easy to find. You must survive and one day seek vengeance," Michael told her solemnly.

"I don't understand, Father. You want me to never return to Aberevon, but if I don't return, how do I have any chance of seeking revenge?"

"Ah, wise girl. This king is mad and will never stop chasing you. He is plagued by poor health. According to Luigi, the man who is helping us, your mother had the power to give King Damien a new lease of life, and as the daughter of a sorceress, the king believes you have that power too. As long as he lives, he will keep searching; he is obsessed. When he does find you, make sure you are ready. Remember what your mother used to tell you: 'Trust no one.'"

"What about you? You don't have anything to tell me beyond run away and never come back?"

"Talia, I know you are upset with me right now, but someday you will understand why I am doing what I am doing."

"Someday? Why not now?" asked Talia.

Michael laughed. "Because, my dear, only when you become a parent will you realise that the well-being and safety of your children always comes before your own. It is a sacrifice that any parent makes with pleasure. The greatest despair for a parent is to stand back and do nothing while a child is hurt. As for my parting advice to you, there is a thin line between being brave and being reckless. Remember which side you want to be on," he said. As Talia turned to leave after one last hug, he whispered, "And one more thing. I will always love you."

CHAPTER XV

How are we to know what lies in the depths of the heart of a terrible beast? It may be a relentless hunger, a need for violence, a thirst for revenge, obedience to the master's command, or even fear. Ultimately, its motives will manifest themselves through its actions. Until then, don't be quick to judge.
Talia

VASSAL TO A RUTHLESS KING—THE DRAGON

THE DRAGON'S CELL, the largest standalone structure of the dungeon, was at the extreme end. Even behind a gigantic iron door fortified and reinforced many times over, the dragon's acute sense of hearing could pick up every footstep clattering on the stone flooring. To the dragon, the footsteps were a death knell, a call to his duties of extermination and doom. Seeing the fear in the eyes of those he was about to kill created a sense of shame and loathing which didn't seem to ever go away.

Damien, however, forced the dragon to lay waste to the armies, cities, castles, granaries and even the homes of his enemies. Startled soldiers would stand frozen, all their defensive manoeuvres laid to waste as the dragon's dark shadow would creep upon them from the skies. Outrunning the fire-spewing dragon proved to be an impossible task, and soon the fiery path created by him would be awash with burned skeletons and ashes of Damien's enemies. Damien's legion of hundreds and thousands of soldiers would follow in the dragon's wake, effortlessly taking control of once powerful empires brought to their knees by the king's killing machine.

He was a powerful dragon but a mere puppet in the hands of his king. When he wasn't reigning over the skies, Damien's dungeon was home to the dragon. It was a brutal assertion to his life of captivity. It lay in the bowels of the Earth and stretched the entire length of the castle. It was witness to the suffering endured by many a prisoner at the hands of the past rulers of Aberevon who, in seclusion, away from the attention of their adoring public, were almost as violent and ruthless as Damien. The dungeon would have been cast in total darkness were it not for the occasional firelight the guards used to drive away the gloom when they were alone in the desolate dungeon. Except, of course, at night because that was when the dragon had dark dreams. He would stay awake all night curled up in a corner hoping that the hallucinatory demons and monsters that had a tendency to float out of the gloom of his own imagination would not see him.

The sight of the ferocious dragon trembling in terror made the guards dissolve into laughter with tears rolling down their cheeks, turning his fear into anger. His deafening roars would shake the very foundations of the castle, abruptly turning their mirth into alarm. King Damien would suddenly emerge in the dungeon, his face black with rage and a special whip in his hand. He would approach the dragon, seemingly uncaring of his own safety, and the mighty creature would do nothing but fall silent in the king's presence. The dragon knew the soldiers in the dungeon gossiped about this. "Does the monstrous dragon think he is a mouse?" they would say to each other. They would jeer at the fact his mighty paws could break the tiny whip into two yet the mere sight of it had him falling silent and cowering in fear. "With one breath, he can burn down our king who approaches him so carelessly, but what does he do? He hides his head between his paws."

The dragon was supposed to be a natural born killer, but he did not feel like one. Violence made him feel nauseated, dizzy and all nasty inside. King Damien's whip unlocked some terrifying, unexplained fear within him, and all rationale withered away at the sight of it. The soldiers could laugh at him, the king could threaten him, but despite it all, the dragon was determined not to be broken. He was King Damien's creature to command, but within himself, he retained a small sliver of dignity that he would always try to hold on to.

Damien was on his way to Syrolt, an island in the North West beyond the mountainous lands and across the Clavoln Sea. The journey across land and sea would have taken the king a fortnight and a half. As it were, astride the dragon, he would cover the same distance in a matter of days. It was the longest journey the dragon had ever undertaken, but the best one of its young life.

For the first time, the dragon felt free. He luxuriated in the sparkle and might of the ocean and he took in the allure of the distant rolling green hills of islands they flew over. Being able to revel in the blue of the morning and to appreciate the inky and mysterious darkness of the night was one of life's simple pleasures he rarely had the opportunity to enjoy. He meant to savour the exultation of flying with his majestically unfurled wings as if it was the very heavens that he explored.

King Damien claimed that the princess of Syrolt once lived in Aberevon. She had been promised to him long ago when she just a girl but had been cruelly snatched away. From the king's victorious rantings after a meeting with his favourite hunter, Garcia, the dragon realized they had been looking for this particular girl for years and years. Now they had finally found her.

The dragon felt sorry for the unknown girl who had been unlucky enough to be hunted down by Garcia, for he both hated and feared Garcia with all his heart. There was some terrible memory in relation to Garcia buried somewhere. Luckily, Garcia stayed away, only throwing the dragon a solitary glance from the corner of his eye.

King Damien planned to abduct the princess and her daughter, and then he intended to unleash the dragon on Syrolt and its people. He wanted the dragon to kill hundreds of innocents without batting an eyelid and to lay to ruins what was a beautiful island country. Not a single soul was meant to survive. The people of Syrolt had the audacity to make the girl who belonged to *him* their princess. She was meant to be King Damien's wife, *his* queen, and above all, *his* salvation from illness and death. They had to pay in blood for their folly of offering sanctuary to *his* blue haired sorceress.

UNBIDDEN, a memory tiptoed into the dragon's thoughts. He, too, had encountered a lady with blue hair a very long time ago. He remembered waking from a deep slumber to find her staring at him. She carried the lifeless body of a little boy in her arms. They were surrounded by Damien's guards, who stood warily some distance away. Were the guards there to protect her from him? Something terrible must have happened to her because the bruises on her arms and neck bore witness to the brutality she must have been subjected to. Her lower lip was swollen from a well-aimed punch, but her injuries were nothing compared to the pain he saw in her eyes. She must have loved the boy very much.

"Why did I not pay heed to the Wraith?" she mumbled to herself again and again. The dragon wanted to soothe her broken spirit, but what comfort could he offer her? As he racked his brain for a way to reach out to her, she addressed him, concern marking her voice.

"Look after yourself," she said as though they knew each other, but he had never seen her before. Why was she concerned about him? He was fine, wasn't he? She was the one who was badly hurt. Before he could ask her what she meant, the guards dragged her away.

"Don't worry; I can take care of myself," he tried to say to her. The guards and the lady had barely left his line of sight when the dungeon became very cold. He remembered hearing the screams of the petrified guards, the sound of them running, and then the loud thuds of them falling to the ground still screaming. From the lady, he heard only whimpers of fear followed by a startled shriek; then all was quiet for a beat. In the silence of the dungeon, he heard the beginning of strange whispers that grated and sent shivers through him. His hackles rose in response to the eerie voices that did not sound quite human.

"You were warned," they said. *"Again, and again, we came to you but you cast our advice away and now you must pay. You used your magic to help the vile king, and all our sacrosanct tenets into the wind you threw away. The price your family has paid and now the turn is yours. The great unknown, the land of the dead, will be your purgatory as still living and breathing you will walk its lonely paths. You ignored the prophecy and so now you are cursed. For all of eternity you can never return."*

"Take me with you; punish me as you must. It is indeed my lot to bear," said the sorceress. "But he is an innocent. I only ask you this. Give him a little time to make things right. Don't take him away," the blue-haired prisoner begged the unknown tormentors.

The voices whispered amongst themselves until they said in unison, *"Only until vengeance is his and not a day longer, otherwise even his soul will no longer exist. When it is time for him to go, you may return to guide him along, but then to your perpetual prison you will return once more."*

The dragon wondered whom they were talking about. Was it about the boy in the lady's arms? Then he'd heard the lady sigh in agreement and he was sure she whispered goodbye. Was it to him, or was there someone else around he hadn't seen?

The dungeon fell so silent, the hissing of his own breath the only sound he heard. He always wondered what had happened, but never fully understood because he never saw the lady or the same guards again.

CHAPTER XVI

*Damien was the hunter and I was the hunted. He was the predator and I
the prey. His men came for me and I ran. Never breathing easy, scared
to sleep, and never able to trust anyone enough to make a single friend.
Was this how the rest of my life would be? Was there anything but fear
and fleeing in my destiny?*
Talia

THE SEARCH FOR SERENITY—TALIA

TALIA CAME upon Syrolt by fluke.

Since fleeing Aberevon, she kept moving. Her sense of foreboding grew each day. She ensured there was randomness to her
selection of a place to move to. The constant moving erased
Talia's teenage sense of wonderment. Yes, strangers could be kind,
but many of them also saw a lone, unaccompanied girl as an

attractive challenge. Fending them off required a great deal of ingenuity and quick thinking. Luckily, her mother had taught her to defend herself, so she had nothing to fear. Still, she missed being a protected, well-loved little girl, but the softness started fading when she met Damien. Evading Damien's many spies and soldiers did not allow for any pathos or sloppiness. They were too many and too well armed to fight off were she to be caught, so she had to match her wits against them instead.

Talia knew that the soldiers were looking for a young, blue haired girl, so she became an old crone, bent with old age walking with the support of a stick. Just a change in posture and walk made her invisible to the searching eyes, her face and hair covered against what seemed were the vagaries of the weather. She learned to avoided patterns, always reminding herself that patterns were traps. She never overstayed or returned to the same place more than once, nor did she buy food from the same area or vendor twice. She spread disinformation here and there on the whereabouts of a blue haired girl from Aberevon, often sending Damien's spies into a tizzy. She avoided inns, always taking shelter in forests or caves. She confided in no one and made no friends, for she instinctively knew that the more people she trusted, the lower her chances of survival.

Talia knew that as things stood, she would not survive another encounter with Damien. She had no intention of giving him what he wanted. She would rather die. She hadn't seen any sign of magic in herself whatsoever. She wanted to laugh at her own destiny. She was being hunted like an animal for capabilities she didn't have.

The toughest part was to be on her guard all the time. She barely slept and often found herself jerking awake in a cold sweat after just a couple of hours. Peace of mind was elusive and everything was taking a toll on her. Talia knew she wouldn't be able to sustain it much longer. She needed to find a place to disappear to and prepare for vengeance. Stability conflicted with being on the run. Despite the distance she had built between her and Aberevon, she never felt safe enough.

Talia was right to worry because the soldiers nearly caught her one day. One of the younger ones caught her hand, trying to befriend a pretty and young local girl. Imagine his surprise when he found himself looking into the startled blue eyes of the girl from his old neighbourhood, the one his king now hunted. Before he could react, Talia gave him a mighty push and in the opposite direction she fled. The young soldier shouted for his colleagues but none were around. He gave chase but, fortunately for Talia, he was too late. She had picked up the scattered belongings of a drunken sailor and, disguising herself as a deckhand, got passage on board a ship bound for ports in the Clavoln Sea.

Talia had no idea where the ship was heading, but as it moved towards the open sea, she felt the last vestiges of her bond with Aberevon break away. Worry for the father she had left behind would torment her until she knew he was alive and well, but the bond she had with the land that had once been her home had been severed by the cold-blooded and callous behaviour of Aberevon's king.

Many weeks later, when Talia saw the island country of Syrolt, she felt a ray of optimism for the first time in a long while. She soon found employment in the nearest village in a local grocery. The owner was a kindly old woman whose children had moved to the mainland a long time ago. Lonely and desperately in need of some help, she accepted Talia's explanation that the land she was from required her to be garbed at all times from head to toe. The young girl was trying to be brave, but the old woman saw the exhaustion and the despair that lined her eyes. She offered Talia lodging in the room above if she agreed to helping out with household tasks. Rising at dawn, Talia would head downstairs to the store. The owner rewarded her hard work and diligence with a modest supper, allowing her some extra funds for the likes of clothes and candles, etc. She didn't mind the frugality, but a life of anonymity without any family or friends was a lonely one for a girl who was once constantly surrounded by love and laughter. However, after life on the run for almost a year, there was plenty of comfort to be found in the sameness and routine of her days.

Often lost in her own thoughts, Talia was completely unaware of how heads turned in her direction. The hard knocks and terror of the past failed to mask her inner radiance and grace. Her sorrow only further accentuated the loveliness of her features and the beauty within. To her admirers, she was the epitome of politeness but nothing more. Despite her loneliness, she forced herself to remain aloof from all overtures of friendship because friends would be curious. In fact, the women were even more eager then the men to learn more about her. The questions were one too many and Talia would often find herself going red in the face trying to hold her tongue.

Almost six months passed before Talia even found the courage to venture out. Once she did, she got into the habit of visiting a tiny chapel quite a distance from the central marketplace that she came upon during her leisurely walks. Most folks preferred to attend service at the main church in town instead of making the inconvenient trek outside of the city to the somewhat derelict and relatively deserted chapel, but Talia didn't mind the long walk in the least. There amidst the chapel's silent, hallowed interiors with the fragrance of burning frankincense and perfumed lilies wafting around her, she found peace. She prayed hard for the souls of her mother and brother, and for the well-being and safety of her father. She also prayed for the strength and the opportunity for vengeance, although she wasn't sure if it was right or not.

After visiting the chapel, she would stroll by the banks of the river, marvelling and committing to memory the beauty of the wild bushes, the colourful flowers and the chirping birds. This freedom meant the world to her.

Once she had absorbed enough to cleanse her soul, Talia would close her eyes, freeing her mind from the beauty around and forcing her thoughts to her worst fear—to Damien. Talia would imagine Damien standing before her as if in flesh and blood spinning tales about her mother and brother, enticing her to go with him. Suppressing the urge to turn and run, she would force herself to breathe again. She would then retrieve her crossbow and sword from the bushes where she had hidden them, the craftsmanship of both so elegant and perfect that they could be considered works of art. In reality, they were deadly and sharp weapons capable of ending a life with the lightest of touches and her last resort against a mad man.

Talia knew Damien would be expecting a sorceress, but he would get only an ordinary girl. Her death would be quick if he learned she had no magic. She had to be prepared if she were to stand any chance at all.

Since her mother disappeared, Talia's combatant skills had grown rusty, but she had learned enough. For a long time, the sword felt stiff and unwieldy in her hands. Her movements were awkward and frozen, but then Talia would imagine a sneering Damien in front of her. *Block him*, she would command herself. *Don't leave yourself wide open to an attack.* She would swing right, imagining Damien coming in from the left, lunging towards her, an evil glint in his eyes. She kept at it, repeating the same manoeuvres again and again until she had perfected them, then adding new ones and repeating the process. The bow, despite being lightweight, felt heavy to her stiff shoulder. The arrows she tried to shoot flew everywhere but at the target. Talia thought it was a grand thing indeed that she hadn't unwittingly killed herself, an innocent animal, or a passer-by. As time went by, the crossbow began to feel familiar once more. The arrows began to find their mark. But she could feel her fear growing every day. How would she seek vengeance when the mere thought of meeting her greatest *and only* foe again choked her and left her paralyzed? What would she do when the time came to face him?

And what of her father? Was he safe? Anxiety for him clouded her thoughts. How would she find him without returning to Aberevon? Worry made her hands tremble. *Focus*, she told herself, once again casting an icy cloak of calmness around herself.

CHAPTER XVII

I thought I had no power, but Mother always had the ability to draw creatures of nature towards her, and now so did I. Joshua feared animals, but not I. There was no animal I did not care for. But most of all, I loved horses because they reminded me of home and all I had lost.
Talia

HE HERO THAT WALKED ON FOUR LEGS
—AHERIN

OUT IN THE woods of Syrolt, Talia drifted along a solitary path she hadn't been down before. She came to a standstill in front of a handsome, reddish brown Arabian horse with a glossy coat and a smooth black mane and tail. The very sight of it brought an onslaught of precious memories as she felt her eyes grow moist. Compared to her pony, Liata, this horse on the river path was much bigger, but Talia was still mesmerised. When it saw Talia, it became restless and looked like it was about to bolt.

Talia soon realized the horse was wearing a saddle with its reins trailing behind, but there was no rider in sight. Before she could speculate on what must have happened, a high-spirited snort from the horse attracted her attention. Her resolve to keep a low profile was quickly forgotten and she approached the horse from its offside in a non-threatening manner, making soft, comforting and crooning sounds. Sensing Talia's presence, the horse rolled its eyes and tried to shy away. She kept up the soothing sounds and gradually it grew less alarmed. Talia now interspaced the sounds she made with soft, calming words. "Come on, boy. Don't be shy. I would never hurt you. Don't you agree that a handsome horse like you deserves some love? Here boy." The Arabian gave an answering sigh in return, and as if finally deciding that she posed no threat, it stood still. Talia stopped by its side and continued speaking softly. As she ran her hand over its coat, she wished she had some sugar cubes or a juicy carrot in her pocket to offer it.

Standing there with her head resting against the horse's flank, Talia could feel the wind on her face and whipping through her hair. She wished she were a stable hand instead of a shop assistant. Just being surrounded by horses, even if it involved mucking them out and cleaning the stables, would have been satisfaction enough for her.

As though driven by the force of her memories, Talia impulsively climbed into the saddle and clasped the reins, telling herself it was just for a little while. For the first time in many months, she felt revived and like her old self again.

With a rider in the saddle, the Arabian became slightly skittish as though eager to get going. Without giving it any thought as she had done it countless times before, Talia applied slight pressure with her legs while leaning forward in the saddle. Before she could even say *go boy*, the horse broke into an elegant trot.

The Arabian galloped like the wind, lifting Talia's spirits, making her feel strong and alive. Singing at the top of her voice, she laughed with exhilaration, thrilling in the deep connection she felt with this powerful creature and the heady sense of freedom it gave her.

As girl and horse finally slowed down, Talia suddenly fell silent as she saw a young man standing to the side grinning in amusement. A startled Talia almost lost her balance. The watching man wore his hair slightly longer than necessary. A few wavy tendrils strayed onto his cheeks but did not seem to bother him in any way. He was lean and tall. He stood under a tree slouching slightly, casually munching an apple. He made no attempt to disguise the humour in his eyes. How could she not fail to note that he had the most beautiful laughing brown eyes she had ever seen? Why was she scrutinizing him in such detail from atop a horse? She had never done anything like this before. What must he make of all this staring? Turning red, Talia dismounted, refusing the courteous hand he held out. Her marked rebuff did not ruffle his composure. He bowed politely to her before addressing the horse in a scolding but affectionate voice. "Aherin, you naughty boy. After all the sugar cubes I fed you, you threw me off like a sack of potatoes and ran off with this pretty young lady."

As Talia spluttered in indignation, he continued. "Is this the way to treat your pr—?" The young man stopped abruptly, almost choking on his apple.

Talia liked the stranger. Anyone would. Everything about him was friendly and open. But since early childhood, her mother had ingrained deep within her the habit of avoiding strangers. No matter if it was the children in the neighbourhood of Aberevon, or customers who tried to chat with her as she attended to them here in Syrolt, she never opened up to others. There was nothing threatening in this young man's demeanour, but she couldn't bring herself to speak to him. It was very difficult to let go of patterns of the past, especially the ones that had saved her life.

Despite the young man's amiable nature, he was hiding something. He had hesitated when he spoke to his horse, Aherin. It seemed she was not the only one with secrets. She should make her exit before he started asking her impertinent questions. Muttering a quick apology, she turned towards the lane and cast one last longing glance at the horse. She was proud that she absolutely did not sneak a peek at the cute young man—however much she wanted to.

Aherin's young master called out to her but thankfully did not give chase. Talia returned to her mundane but safe life. What was it he had called after her? *"I don't even know your name."* Talia did not know his name either. Such a pity. At least she knew the name of the horse.

As he stood there holding Aherin's reins, Aiden, Crown Prince of Syrolt, shook his head in wonder. The girl had accomplished a feat he'd had limited success with—befriending Aherin and riding him like an expert equestrian. In his book, not falling off Aherin for an extended period qualified as expertise.

What a wonderful girl.

Such spirit and beauty.

CHAPTER XVIII

Nothing in life is ironclad. I decided I would never open my heart again, but all it took was a horse, a man and a boy, and I was lost. They saved me when I didn't even know I needed saving.
Talia

GLIMPSE OF POWER—TALIA

OVER THE NEXT FEW DAYS, Aiden thought a lot about *her*, the beautiful girl who refused to share her name. It didn't matter who she was or where she came from; he just wanted to see her again. Syrolt was an island, but it wasn't small. Where would he even start looking for her?

Why had the girl run away as soon after she saw him? Did she have a possessive boyfriend or a mean father she was afraid of? Had he terrified her? He ought to stay away, but he knew better than to look for someone who didn't want to be found. She seemed like the kind of girl who cherished her privacy. Maybe if he were lucky, he would see her again.

Aiden was well aware that his sister, Andrea of Calhem, was hoping he would fall in love with her sister-in-law, Lady Ellie. He liked Ellie but he never really thought about her unless she was standing right in front of him. *Her*, on the other hand, Aiden could not stop thinking about.

ONE DAY, Talia walked back into Aiden's life, and it was all thanks to his nephew, Jesse. During the visit of the royal family of Calhem, Jesse took it in his head to ride Aherin without informing Aiden or the stable hand. No sooner had Jesse mounted the Arabian than he realized he had taken on more than he could handle. All his attempts to rein in the headstrong horse failed and he was reduced to holding on for dear life as Aherin galloped out of the palace gates. An alert gardener warned the palace. Fearing that Jesse may be hurt, Aiden immediately organized search parties.

Meanwhile, Aherin, finding himself master instead of the unschooled and green Jesse, decided to head to the path by the river. He was on the lookout for Talia.

Hours passed with no sign of the little boy. Aiden, who had spent the entire day searching the woods, was riding out again when he was met by a sight he would never forget.

News of the young prince's disappearance had spread and a large crowd had gathered to show support and to pray. Suddenly, murmurs spread through the gathered crowd as they glimpsed Jesse mounted on Aherin. Once he understood that Jesse was only dishevelled but unharmed, Aiden only had eyes for *her* as she focussed on calming Aherin, who was becoming agitated by the growing cheers and applause. She was even more beautiful than he recalled. Fearing a terrible scolding, the recalcitrant boy clung to Talia on dismounting, preventing her from making the unobtrusive escape she was hoping for.

Hidden by the throng of cheering people, Aiden could see the need to flee in Talia's eyes. She was a runner. No wonder Aherin had an affinity for her. They both had that in common. Whatever her reasons, the girl had a good heart. She craved anonymity but she had still put her responsibility for Jesse's safety above her own desires. If only she wouldn't run away this time and give him a chance.

Meanwhile, tears of remorse, relief and happiness flowed freely and Jesse was forgiven—for the moment.

Aherin led them to Syrolt's royal palace. When a bewildered Talia wondered why, Jesse told her whose horse Aherin was. She finally learned his name. Aiden—Prince Aiden. As she reconciled herself to the reality that the only man she had ever liked was royalty, she had to laugh at the fact that she'd run from a king only to fall for a prince. But there was no comparison between Aiden and Damien. The realization that just how much she liked him hit her like a ton of bricks. When she saw him looking oh so solemn and worried for his nephew, the fierce joy she felt took her by surprise. She had not realized just how much she wanted to see him again. Talia knew that he was staring at her, but she could not make herself meet the intensity of those alluring eyes of his. Until she got a better control of her emotions, she would do best to avoid him.

TALIA DIDN'T dare tell Jesse's family of the narrow escape he'd had. Seeing Aherin galloping past, she had initially tried to hide, thinking that his handsome master was the rider, but the sight of the much smaller figure had alerted her to the possibility of danger. She gave chase as Aherin galloped straight towards the edge of the river. Talia was too far away to grab his reins. A deeper instinct took over. She reached out to the Arabian through her thoughts. In her mind, he was right beside her. *"Stop, Aherin. Stop, otherwise the boy will die,"* she pleaded with the horse in a firm voice.

When Talia opened her eyes, it was to the amazing sight of a stationary horse. Aherin was galloping towards the river at break-neck speed when the voice he loved so much reached out to him. He sensed her gentle presence and had no choice but to come to a standstill when she asked. He actually ceased his frenzied ride after checking his speed, slowing down to a gentle trot so that his rider wouldn't suddenly fall off. Talia's anxiety for his little passenger had now become his own.

"Good boy," Talia mumbled.

Jesse lost his precarious hold on Aherin's reins and almost fell into the water, but Talia was there to catch him. Even as she spoke to Aherin, she continued running towards them, so when Jesse fell, it was only into the safety of her arms.

"Where did you come from?" he asked.

"I was right behind you, laddie. You were too scared to see me."

Jesse seemed to be in shock. Talia encased his cold hands in her own and began rubbing them in earnest. After a while, she asked him if he wanted to return home. The boy nodded his head in relief until a terrifying thought struck him. "Will you be sending me back all by myself with this devil?" he stuttered, shuddering in fear.

In Talia's eyes, Aherin was a darling and as harmless as Liata, but she understood where the terror in the Jesse's eyes came from. "There is nothing to be scared of. He is not as scary as he pretends to be," she said, but the little boy still looked unconvinced.

"Aherin is a friend of mine. He will listen to me; have no fear. Whenever you fall, you should get right back in the saddle, other-wise your fear will only grow. So how about you ride him and I walk by your side? I will have his reins in my hand. I won't allow him to run away again."

Talia hoisted Jesse back onto Aherin, and, patting the horse, she said, "Home, Aherin. Walk." It seemed enough for Aherin, who set off at an extremely docile pace. Talia understood how Aherin could be scary; he had thrown off his own master, hadn't he? She just happened to have a soft spot for him—the horse, or the master, or both.

Talia followed Aherin's lead, letting her mind wander to how she had been able to command Aherin from afar. How had this been possible? Had it been the magic her father had told her about? He had told her there was magic within her and it may emerge at the right time. What would have happened if she had been unable to talk to Aherin? She shuddered to even think about it.

CHAPTER XIX

Mother, when I experienced the richness of love, the initial euphoria that one can't get enough of, I understood what you felt when you met Father. It is love that is holding me back and keeping me from moving on. We cannot help who or how we love. Love is a gift, one that is received even if not always asked for.
Talia

GIVING LIFE A CHANCE—TALIA

PRINCESS ANDREA WAS DEEPLY grateful and refused to let Talia leave, insisting that she stay on as an esteemed guest. Talia couldn't ignore such genuine warmth. It felt churlish to refuse, so she finally conceded to stay a while.

Talia developed a close bond with Andrea and Ellie over the

next few weeks. They surrounded her in a circle of such unconditional love that she had no choice but to reciprocate.

After a long time, Talia felt her fears abate. Syrolt was beginning to feel comfortable, like a second skin. She could see herself
living on this island safe and secure, never having to leave. It had
been so long since she'd experienced the warmth and security of a
real home. Then there was Jesse. He followed her everywhere,
reminding her of Joshua so much that sometimes she forgot he
was Andrea's son and not her brother. She couldn't help but laugh
and smile when she was with him.

The one she instinctively tried to avoid was Aiden. She felt
helpless in front of him, as though he could read her mind, but it
would seem rude to avoid him, so she gradually overcame her
shyness and doubts. He was confident but not cocky, sweet but
not cloying, protective but not possessive. Talia tried to ignore
him but she couldn't help but like him. *What is the secret that terri-
fies you?* he seemed to ask her without saying a word. He often
looked at her as though he wanted to protect her. At other times,
he looked as though she was his knight in shining armour.
Without saying a single word, he managed to convey his feelings.

Seeing how good Aiden was with Jesse warmed the cockles of
Talia's heart, and seeing how bad he was with Aherin made her
laugh like nothing else could. Every time she saw Aiden trying to
mount Aherin unsuccessfully, she would burst into peals of laughter, much to his dismay. Then repentance for her casual behaviour
would force her to feel sorry for Aiden and the way Aherin
completely ignored him. As she tried her best to help build
bridges between the man and his reluctant mount, she realized
that maybe he had figured the secret to this girl's heart was
through his stubborn, wilful, one of a kind horse.

When the talk became less about the horse and more about
her, Talia understood Aiden's true feelings, and she was scared.
Not of him but of the way she felt. Now that she knew she felt the
same way too, the temptation to stay was overpowering, but it

wouldn't be fair to Aiden or his family. This was just a dream. She could not forget who was coming for her. Today, tomorrow, or even in ten years. King Damien would come, then what of her friends and this island? Wouldn't she be putting them in danger? She should leave soon if she cared about them. Life with a prince would be far from anonymous. She would put him in danger by choosing to be a part of his life.

"I will spell trouble for you and Syrolt as my enemy is King Damien, the king of Aberevon. He is not quite sane and he has been hunting me for a long time. He will find me one day, Aiden, and then his wrath will rain down on all of us. That is the reason I keep moving. I have already overstayed my welcome here. I should leave on the next ship if I really love you," she told him.

Aiden stared at her in amazement. "Did you hear what just you said?" he asked in disbelief.

"I said I need to leave."

"No. That is not what I heard. You said you love me. Do you think I can let you go after knowing how you feel? I have been madly in love with you since the day I first saw you. To know that you feel the same way...I have no words," said Aiden.

"Yes, *Prince* Aiden, I did say I love you. But what is love? What can it do? My family was full of love, but today my mother and brother are dead. What did love do? It made my mother weak. It broke my father's heart. For the sake of love, he refused to escape with me. He may be dead or imprisoned for all I know. I lost everything in the blink of an eye all in the name of love. And now you want me to willingly put your whole family and country in the eye of a coming storm so that I can have countless more deaths laid at my feet. Is that what you want? Did you not hear anything else I said? I spoke of Damien, my nemesis, a powerful king. He is not like you. He uses any means necessary to get what he wants. Why do you need one more enemy? Don't you have enough of your own?"

"I don't know what to say, Talia," he said, his eyes full of sorrow. "How do I convince you that none of this matters except the way we feel about each other?"

"I have worked very hard for the past couple of years to save myself from Damien's goons. I have been preparing for the day I will face him again. If you come into my life, you with your beautiful heart, your kind eyes and your wonderful family, you will make me weak, and I can't allow that to happen. I will leave on the first ship out tomorrow," she said defiantly.

"I can't make you change your mind. If you must go, I won't stop you, but can you give me a chance? Wait six months. I will keep my distance. I will give you your space. When you are ready, I will be waiting. I also make a commitment to you, Talia. This is the word of an honourable man. Your enemy is mine, and if you wish, I will stand before you and fight him. But when the time comes, if you think that no one should face him but you, I will not be your weakness. I will not stop you. I will be your strength and stand with you, or even behind you," said Aiden passionately.

Talia couldn't run away after a confession of love and devotion like that.

JESSE'S PARENTS returned to Calhem but the young prince stayed in Syrolt. Life on the mainland was quite different from island life. He loved the fishing, the boat rides, the beautiful view, and most of all, the visits he and Aherin made to Talia. Aiden never accompanied them. By sending Jesse and Aherin, his message to Talia was clear. The bond between them remained, but the next move was hers. Jesse never mentioned his uncle, and Talia couldn't muster the courage to ask about him. Aiden couldn't make it any clearer. He had said his part. The next move had to come from her.

Six months drew to a close. With a heavy heart, Talia realized she had always known the right thing to do was to leave. She was broken. She had sworn revenge. Aiden didn't need such complications in his life. She was a witness to what marrying a sorceress could do to your life.

She hadn't seen anyone in weeks. Jesse and Aherin had stopped visiting for what she assumed was in anticipation of her impending departure. Goodbyes were tough but she was Michael and Caitlin's daughter; she hadn't been raised a coward. Squaring her shoulders, she set off towards the palace. But something was wrong. As she headed towards the royal headquarters, she realized that the usually bustling island wore a deserted look. There were pockets of soldiers and guards posted everywhere. The palace gates were tightly shut. The soldiers eyed this strangely dressed girl at the gates with suspicion.

Talia was usually so cut off from people that she hadn't realized something was afoot. Syrolt's usual serenity had been replaced with an air of mourning and anticipation as though everyone on the island was holding their breath in unison, waiting, but for what? Talia experienced a deep sense of foreboding. Something told her that it was nothing good. She ran back home to her landlady. The kindly old woman stared at her for a long while.

"I was wondering if you knew?" she said.

"Knew what?" Talia asked. "Please tell me quickly. You are scaring me."

"Calhem was attacked by a neighbouring lord. Prince Aiden has gone to the rescue with half the troops of Syrolt. This was ten days ago. After he joined in, things became more favourable for Calhem, but…" said the landlady.

"But what?" asked Talia, trying to nudge her ahead. Her dread had built up to such an extent that she felt almost faint.

"Prince Aiden has been reported missing for the past four days. Today is the fifth day. As each day passes, hope for his survival diminishes further. Our lady, his sister, Princess Andrea, is almost mad with grief. She spends all her time praying. Prince Jesse has refused to leave his room."

As the kind old lady spoke, understanding shining in her eyes, Talia's sense of detachment increased. It couldn't be. They had to be talking about someone else. Her happy, laughing prince would never go to war, and if he did, surely no one would hurt him? She was fooling herself. The reality wouldn't change just because she wanted it to. Hadn't she experienced enough of the wickedness human beings were capable of?

Talia rushed to the harbour to watch every ship that came in. Days passed. She would remain at her post from the early hours of the morning until dark, and then return the next day to resume her vigil.

Almost a month had passed since her deadline to leave. It meant nothing to Talia anymore. All she was waiting for was news of Aiden's return. She hardly ate, barely slept, and then one day she found herself unable to make her daily pilgrimage to the harbour. She was drastically ill. Exhaustion and delirium kept her confined to bed, her body bathed in sweat and her mind overcome with dark dreams. She kept calling out to Aiden in her sleep.

It was a week before her eyes opened late one night. There was a storm raging outside the window, but for the first time, she felt a sense of calmness and contentment. All was right with her world. Where did this feeling stem from?

The trees swayed riotously, but it was not the majesty of the storm that drew her attention but the sight of the silent figure by the window watching nature's frenzied dance and highlighted by the flashes of lightning that cut through the darkness. Aiden was back. Relief flooded through Talia.

"You landlady let me in," Aiden said. "She seemed to think you wouldn't mind. I had to see you. But if you would like me to, I will leave."

"Don't," said Talia. "I have something to say to you."

"Then speak up, please. Let me hear it. I am afraid I can't take the not knowing anymore," said Aiden.

"I don't want your protection, nor do I need you to save me," Talia said to Aiden. He stiffened hearing her words. *So this is how a rejection sounds.* But then her tone turned softer, more loving. "I only need your love." Almost stumbling on her unsteady feet, Talia fell into his arms. She had made up her mind. "I am not going anywhere. I am yours from this day onwards." The stunned expression on Aiden's face made her ask if he had changed his mind.

"Changed my mind?" Aiden exclaimed, turning towards her and embracing her. "I've thought of nothing else but you for the past seven months. Do you know how often I almost reached your doorstep? When Calhem was attacked, the distraction was almost a relief."

It was not easy for Talia to let go of habits of the past. She was so used to a solitary life, but Aiden was extremely understanding. He reminded her so much of her father. As one day blurred into the next, the darkness of the days gone by began to fade, but the memories and scars were never forgotten. Over time, she locked them up in a little corner of her mind, and before she knew it, Talia found herself richer than she had been for a long time. It was not the title of princess she counted; it was the family she had gained. She welcomed the sunshine and exultation of her new life with a light heart even though she knew Damien would one day return. In the meantime, she wouldn't keep her life on hold.

CHAPTER XX

Being a mother made you strong, but it also made you weak. You were willing to do anything to protect your children, including abandon the man you loved and destroying yourself. There was nothing you wouldn't do to protect your children, and in the end, that became your downfall. Father did tell me that I would only understand his extreme motivation to keep me safe at all costs the day I became a parent. So true...
Talia

HE PAST CATCHES UP—TALIA

TALIA WATCHED six-year-old Katie playing in the damp soil of the garden without a care in the world. All children deserve this care-free time to grow up happy and secure. Her own childhood had initially been happy too, largely because of Joshua. He was and always would be an integral part of her life. Her memories of him were bittersweet, bringing both joy and sorrow, but she would never let go. He never got the chance at life that he deserved. Talia, on the other hand, had been blessed. Was it fair? Why couldn't she have been the one to be taken? It was now ten years since she had left Aberevon. As each new year dawned, she expected King Damien and his hunters to appear in her life, but nothing of that sort had happened. Was he dead? Had he forgotten about her?

Eight wonderful years with Aiden, and now there was Katie too. *Keep Damien away a little while longer,* she pleaded with the gods. *Katie is so small.* Only when Katie was born could she actually empathize with the worry and fears that must have dominated her mother's thoughts. Talia no longer blamed Caitlin for running away. There were so many days when she wanted to pick up Katie, take Aiden's hand, and disappear to some corner of the Earth where no one could find them. But her mother's experience had taught her a lesson. There was no point in running. It was better to stand her ground and be prepared.

Meanwhile, she wanted her little girl to have a perfect life. Caitlin had made the same wish for Talia, but destiny proved it had alternative plans. Now Talia could feel the cruel knock of fate on her own door as a grating, masculine voice abruptly broke through her musing.

"What unusual hair," a man's voice said.

Talia felt fear coursing through her. Katie's lovely blue locks, a replica of Talia's own hair, were uncovered today, the one visible proof of their heritage. She turned slowly to find a smallish but well built ordinary looking man standing before her. He was apologetic for his intrusion, or at least pretended to be.

"My lady, I am a visitor to your splendid island. Lost in its natural beauty, I seem to have mistakenly wandered here," he said, staring blatantly at Katie.

Talia knew a barefaced lie when she heard one. His smile was repugnant to her. Long since had she learned to read a person by their eyes. His were vigilant, watching her with a burning and frightening intensity. They made her uncomfortable and nervous. But why should she be afraid? He was the intruder. Hoping that her anxiety was not visible, she requested him to leave.

"Yes, indeed. I have found what I was looking for." Smiling insolently, he cast another telling glance at Katie's hair. That one look was enough. It confirmed Talia's suspicions. This man had not wandered upon them by mistake. Damien must have been searching for her all these years, and now he had found her.

Talia knew that her past would catch up. She had been waiting for it. She believed she was always ready. Here was a stranger crumbling all her illusions with just a few words and glances. Was Aberevon the place he was returning to? Was Damien his king?

The man was baiting her to ask the question. She ought not to fall into the trap, but she had to know. She had to find out if he was Damien's spy.

"Where are you from? What is your name?" she asked.

The man laughed. "I think the time for games is over, sorceress," he said. "My name is Garcia. That won't mean anything to you, but this will. I am the man who found your mother for King Damien." He grinned at her, making her stomach turn. "Now I've found you, there is only the small matter of making you come with me."

"This is now my home," Talia said. "You can't make me go anywhere with you."

"Oh, I have my ways. I can be very creative," he told her. "First, let me ask you a question. Are you your mother's daughter?"

"What kind of question is that?" asked Talia, confused by the turn in the conversation.

"Your mother was willing to do anything to save your brother. What will you do to save your daughter?" he sneered at Talia.

Talia tried to maintain an air of indifference, and she largely succeeded except for failing to mask the shiver that ran down her spine. It did not go unnoticed and Garcia's gloating smile only widened. "How about this?" asked Talia trying to control her panic. "We leave her behind and I return with you alone." He was right; the time for pretensions and patience was well past. Talia needed to get her vengeance, but first, she had to protect Katie. If she went with him, she could get her vengeance at the same time, maybe keep war from coming to Syrolt. To keep Syrolt, its people and her family safe, she was willing to do anything.

"I need that little girl too," he said, decimating all her plans in one go.

"That *little girl* is my daughter and she is not going anywhere," declared Talia firmly. With the threat to Katie clear, Talia's thinly held composure slowly unravelled. She could try to fight him but she remembered her father's advice: *there is a thin line between being brave and being reckless.* She decided to err on the side of caution. Giving up all pretences of calmness, she began frantically calling for the guards.

Garcia remained unperturbed. He took a quick step forward while keeping an eye on Talia and trying to pre-empt her next move. She was ready for him. He would try to grab Katie; she was sure of it. Garcia knew that if he got his hands on the child, the sorceress would follow him to the ends of the Earth. He bent down towards Katie, but Talia stepped in between the two of them and pushed Katie behind her. Her move disoriented him slightly, enough for her to take advantage of his momentary distraction. She gave him a shove, putting all her weight behind it. Garcia was a heavy man, so wasn't knocked off his feet, but he did flounder and lose his balance.

"Run to the palace, Katie," Talia yelled to the sobbing child. The little girl hesitated, reluctant to leave her mother alone at the mercy of the terrifying looking man. Garcia took advantage of her hesitation by trying to grab her again, but she was more alert this time and neatly stepped out of the way. A wave of adrenaline coursed through her veins as she stepped forward, kicking his leg hard and then pushing him again. This time, the spy careened backwards into a thorn filled rose bush. As he fell, he grabbed at

Katie's hair, making the child howl in pain. He gave a grunt of satisfaction as he looked at the blue strands of hair in his hand.

"How dare you hurt my daughter!" screamed Talia, and using her feet as a weapon, she began kicking Garcia. The thorns in the bush pricked and ruptured his skin every time he tried to roll over or rise, making his escape from the angry Talia very difficult. He tried to grab her ankle and pull her down but she kept moving. Katie stopped crying and stood staring at her mother dancing around. She had seen Talia riding Aherin and at swordplay, also with a bow and arrow, but never like this looking like an angry, avenging goddess.

Garcia had bulk on his side. Talia knew she could have tried to fight him if she was alone, but she couldn't risk Katie getting hurt. Seeing Garcia quite badly entangled in the mass of the thorns, Talia grabbed Katie and started running towards the palace. She knew he could easily catch her if he chose to give chase. She was banking on the fact that a degree of self-preservation would encourage him to beat a hasty retreat.

Katie was silent. Was she hurt or merely in shock? Talia wanted to call out to her but she was already quite out of breath. She had to gulp mouthfuls of air just to keep running. All the shoving, kicking, running, and carrying Katie was taking its toll on Talia. She twisted her head and looked behind hoping that Garcia would be gone.

The man was right behind her. "I am the king's best hunter," he shouted at her. Luckily for her, he was short, otherwise he would have surely grabbed Katie by now. "I am the one who killed your brother, and if you don't stop, I will kill you." Talia gave a sharp cry of pain. She didn't know if it was because the man spoke of Joshua so casually or because the agonizing jab close to her right shoulder blade warning her that he was armed and not above using weapons to stop her. He must have thrown a knife at her. She could feel it protruding from her shoulder. She staggered, holding on tight to Katie. "Hold on to me, Katie," she whispered.

Talia was falling. She used her hand to cushion Katie's head while twisting slightly as they toppled. Her body broke the little girl's contact with the ground. Talia was now too exhausted to run. The weakness she felt was fast spreading. Frantically running her hands over Katie, Talia saw that she was scared but relatively unhurt. Whispering reassuring words, she covered the sobbing girl's little body with her own. The spy was going to have to go through her to reach Katie. Talia did not intend to let go of her little girl. She could hear him. Soon he would be upon them.

"Mama, why are you crying?" the little girl asked finally. "Let us hide. The bad man is coming," Katie whispered.

Talia gave a small cry of relief. Why hadn't she thought of that? There were no places for them to hide for a length of time, but she couldn't run anymore. There could be no greater foolishness than standing injured with a child in tow in plain sight. With Katie holding her hand, Talia half limped and half crawled to a wall swarming with a multitude of exotic creepers. If she survived this, she would give the gardener a hug for installing this monstrosity in the garden. The wall wasn't much of a buffer, though. Garcia only had to take a few steps ahead and look back over his shoulder and he would spot them.

The throbbing pain kept increasing in waves and then cresting. Even though she could not see it, she felt the blood dripping down her back. The stinging she could ignore, but the spams that had started in her arm would make carrying Katie difficult. Talia felt her legs getting weaker. She wouldn't even be able to run soon. It looked like she was out of options and that confronting Garcia was the only one that remained.

Garcia was armed and Talia was weaponless. She had a little girl to protect and he seemed to have nothing to lose. The odds against her were mounting. She had to even the playing field a bit. Could Katie do it? "Katie, I need your help to deal with his man. Can you help me?" *How?* Talia could see the question form on the lips of her little girl.

"I need you to do two very important things. First, there is some sort of dagger in Mama's shoulder. It should be similar to the one cousin Jesse has. Do you remember it? He shouted at you when he found you playing with it. You cried for hours that day," Talia said.

Katie nodded her head sagely, the memory bringing a frown to her face. "Katie, listen to me. I need you to slowly pull this thing out from my shoulder. It will be difficult, so you may want to give it all your strength. If my shoulder starts bleeding, use this to stop it," said Talia, trying to tear out bits from her sleeve.

"Wait, Mama, I have a better idea," said Katie, and she ran out before Talia could stop her. Where had the child gone? Talia could feel the rising panic, but when she looked up, there stood Katie carefully holding the edges of her skirt filled with delicate pink yarrow flower clusters, their sweet fragrance mingling with the pungent and spicy aroma of their fern-like feathery leaves. "The physician told me these leaves help with bleeding because I keep falling down nearly every day. They were right next to the asters," Katie said smiling.

Despite the pain she was in and the danger of being discovered any minute, Talia couldn't help marvelling at the foresight of her daughter, but before that the dagger could be removed, Talia had one more thing to tell Katie. "Katie, after you pull out the dagger, I need you to give it to me and then run and hide. Bundle up and take cover in a thick bush. Don't come out, no matter what the man says or does. He mustn't find you at any cost, otherwise he will take you away from us."

"What about you?" Katie asked. "You are hurt."

"I am still your mother and it is my job to protect you. I will deal with him, but I need you to hide. Pull it out now, Katie. Close your eyes if you are scared."

Katie stepped behind Talia and put her shaking hands on the handle of the knife for was not a dagger but a knife with a pearl handle. But the little girl's hands were slippery and her efforts did not yield any result other than to cause Talia extreme pain. "On more time, Katie, and then you have to go and hide," said Talia. Katie went back to trying, and this time, Talia managed to stretch one hand behind and help her. Between the two of them, the knife was soon out and then Katie was smearing the wound with the flowers and leaves. "Go, now," Talia said weakly. I'll hold them in place."

Barely had Katie crept out and stepped to the other side of the wall—thankfully out of sight—when Talia felt a large hand grip her arm and she found herself looking into the blazing eyes of Garcia. "Where is the girl?" he growled.

"Gone!" she screamed, plunging the knife into his hand while kicking him n the stomach and poking the fingers of her free hand into his right eye. "How dare you hurt Joshua! You deserve to die." Garcia was yelling in pain but Talia saw his left hand rise, a hunting dagger in it. She grabbed Garcia's raised arm and pushed it towards his own side. As the dagger sank into his skin, he gave a loud cry of anger and pain.

Talia saw defeat in his eyes but she knew it was fleeting. "King Damien will come for you on his dragon. This island of yours will be a shell of dust, ash and stones. He will come and he will take you back to Aberevon. But don't worry; you won't be alone, for he will take your daughter too."

Talia was in tremendous pain but through it, she felt her panic and anger grow. *How dare he threaten her and Syrolt this way!* The air around her began to pulsate with a fierce energy. One moment Garcia was standing in front of her, his painful boasts emerging from his loud mouth, and the next he was lying at least ten feet away, thrown back by a powerful and invisible force. Talia stared at the fallen man. *What just happened? Who flung him away?* What was it her father had said? *Your powers would surface when you are angry or upset.* Any magic that flowed from her was linked to her emotions. Using her powers, she had flung Garcia like a rag doll. Now Damien would never believe that she knew no magic.

Before the stupefied Garcia could react, Talia heard pounding on the cobblestones. Turning, she saw the most beautiful sight in the world—the Syrolt colours of green and blue. Help was here. Talia heard a bellow of rage behind her. Garcia was limping and running but fast fading out of sight as he ran towards the sea as fast as he could. He must already have a boat waiting to take him to a ship. He would warn King Damien, who would want to add Katie to his collection of sorceresses. Garcia had to be stopped at any cost. But it was too late because the guards first stopped to check on Talia. She tried to tell them to catch Garcia before he escaped, but she no longer sounded coherent. The ache in her shoulder was now unbearable. "He's getting away!" she screamed. "Please, don't let him get away. Find Katie."

The guards barely heard her as she slipped away into oblivion.

DAMIEN HAD LOOKED for Talia for a long, long time. Believing he was in love, he had decided to wait for her rather than wed another. There were many sightings but no success until Garcia reached Syrolt ten years after Talia bolted from Aberevon.

As Damien headed to Syrolt on the back of his dragon, he realized just how much he was looking forward to seeing Talia again. He hoped she was still as afraid of him as she had been all those years ago. The healing Caitlin had worked on him had long faded and his health was fast deteriorating.

Talia would regret her decision to marry another. If she weren't already petrified of him, arriving on the dragon would help her take the leap from faith to fear. If only she knew who she would actually be facing.

Maybe, to make it more fun, Damian just may tell her the truth about the dragon. It would make the chase and the capture all the more exciting.

CHAPTER XXI

*Now I know the true meaning of love, it means having everything
to lose.*
Talia

𝒯HE WAITING GAME—TALIA AND KING DAMIEN

DAMIEN WAS COMING FOR HER. If that wasn't terrifying enough, he
had a mighty dragon at his command. Nevertheless, it was time to
take a stand, time to stop hiding and face him. The more she ran,
the more she feared him. She was no longer the scared girl she
used to be, but neither was she a powerful sorceress like her
mother. Her magic had made rare appearances only in situations
of extreme peril and urgency or when she was extremely angry or
upset. It was the same powerful force that had thrown the ruthless
Garcia away from her. It was also magic that had allowed her to

reach Aherin. But what would Damien do with a sorceress with such strong but uncontrolled powers?

Ever since the incident with Aherin and Jesse, Talia had tried to resurrect her powers. She had faked anger and shown real frustration but nothing happened. It was only when Garcia showed up that the magic surfaced once more.

All of this meant only one thing: she would be standing against a dragon as a mortal with unreliable powers. It was no longer just her life on the line. The future of Syrolt and all its inhabitants were at stake; this much she knew.

Aiden was very protective of Katie that Talia was reminded of her father. She would have loved for her father to have met Aiden. When she fled from Aberevon, she had truly believed she had lost it all, but with Aiden, she had learned to give life another chance.

Talia decided Aiden must stay away from Damien and the dragon at all costs. "I lost the guidance and love of both of my parents very early on. I refuse to let the same thing happen to Katie. She needs at least one of us. Besides, Damien will come after her too. You cannot protect both of us. You must stay with her," she told him.

"I will send her to my sister. She will be safe there. I need to be with you," Aiden insisted.

"Damien will kill anyone other than me on sight. You can send a hundred soldiers, but if what we have heard from our own spies is true, they will all be killed. I am the one Damien needs alive. Once I kill the dragon, Damien is all yours," said Talia.

"Are you asking me to stand back and watch while you fight a dragon and a despicable killer all alone?" Aiden asked incredulously, not knowing if he should be upset, shocked or proud of her.

"Do you remember what I told you long ago when you returned from Calhem?" she asked.

"Is this a test?" he laughed. "Yes, I do. You said you wanted my love not my protection. Even then, you knew this day would come and you were preparing me for it, weren't you?" he murmured incredulously.

"I did warn you that the trouble chasing me was mine alone. If Syrolt, its people and our family are hurt in any way on my account, what will I do? How will I feel about being the sole cause of so much death and destruction? You and the army must stand back. I don't know if I will be successful, so you will have to be prepared to deal with the worst in case I fail," Talia admitted. She didn't want to give him false hope.

"That would never happen," Aiden assured her confidently. "You have been waiting for this day, preparing for it since the time you left Aberevon. Why would you fail? But what if he just whisks up you and flies away on this dragon?" asked Aiden. He wasn't quite sure if he was deadly serious or joking; after all, he had never seen a dragon. Could one actually be coming to Syrolt?

"Protect Katie and the people. As long as there is hope, I will find a way back to you. But you must not follow me or leave Katie alone. Until Damien is dead, she will always be in danger. I've been happy all these years but never free. I knew Damien would never stop looking for me. The temporary respite I had came to an end the day his hunter found me. Let me face my past. Its power over me has to end one way or the other so that I can truly move on."

Talia had always appreciated and admired Aiden's positivity, but in the days ahead, she learnt to value him even more. Once convinced that facing her nemesis was something she had to do alone, he devoted his energy to helping her rather than complaining.

∾

TALIA CHOSE the large maze just beyond the palace gardens for her confrontation with Damien and the dragon. Its layout was extremely familiar to her. It would offer her the benefit of an element of surprise as well as a few hiding places; it was also reasonably far from the palace. She was counting on the partnership between her and Aherin to draw the dragon away from Damien's watchful eye.

Talia still had the weapons her father gave her a long time ago. She had always oiled, polished, waxed, and sanded them. Aiden had added to her collection over the years. A crossbow, a falchion sword, a broadsword—a twin of his own sword—and a lightweight lance that could be used as a projectile. Which one of these weapons would be best suited to bringing down a dragon? She wasn't quite sure of the answer to that one.

Aiden would spend hours in the palace grounds and in the maze practising various manoeuvres with her. Everyone was willing to help in whatever way they could. Talia took all the help she needed. Too much was hinging on her success. She knew that, ultimately, she would be facing Damien alone, but now was not the time to stand on pride. Help offered must be taken, especially if it took her closer to her ultimate goal.

"Be careful; you and Katie are all I have," Aiden said again and again in the coming days. He believed in her, but that did not stop him from being concerned. He often looked like he had something more to add but words seemed to fail him. The sorrow in his eyes, though, told Talia their own story.

Falling short of words to express his love, Aiden finally held Talia in his arms as they stared out into the distant maze. In this familiar circle of security and love, they forgot the fear and uncertainty that lay ahead, at least for a while.

Talia knew she could kill Damien without the slightest bit of hesitation. He had ravaged her family after all. But her parents had always taught her to only love and respect the individuality and majesty of every creature. True that the dragon was a killer spreading mayhem, chaos and death, but it had always been on

Damien's command. The dragon was a creature of God, supernatural or not. *Will I be able to harm him? By the time I make up my mind, the dragon will probably have burned me with its flaming hot breath*, thought Talia. *I won't need to make a decision at all.* She made up her mind. She would be prepared but she would take the final call depending on how the confrontation went. There was no question; if it came to a choice between her family and the dragon, she would have to protect her family.

Talia spent as much as time as she could with Aiden and Katie. Anticipating the worst, she also appealed in secret for help from Andrea and Ellie in Calhem.

Ultimately, it came down to the waiting. Days became weeks, and it was now almost two months since she had seen the hunter from Aberevon. The doubts began to creep in.

Just when her anxiety reached unimaginable levels and she was almost planning to break her promise to her father and return to Aberevon, anything to bring an end to this waiting, the alarms were sounded. The dragon had been spotted. There was no time to be lost.

As Talia slipped on the lightweight armour that Aiden had specially crafted for her, she reflected on how she was always saying goodbye. Every time she found happiness, it was time to face the next challenge. Irrespective of whether she survived this one, she was thankful for the wonderful memories she had with her parents and Joshua and with Aiden and Katie and the rest of their family.

With a final shake of her head, Talia discarded her helmet. She was going to face Damien in all her glory. She wasn't going to hide her true self. She was going to look him in the eye. Damien was arriving on a fire-breathing dragon, wasn't he? Well, he would find himself facing a warrior princess astride a monstrous Arabian. She and Aherin, the two of them together, were going to channel all of their courage and ferocity to bring Damien down.

Carefully keeping her true emotions reigned in, Talia hugged and kissed the sleepy Katie.

"Where are you going?" Katie asked, suddenly wide awake.

"Mama has something important to do. I will try to be back soon," Talia said, holding back her tears.

"Has the dragon arrived?" Katie asked, startling Talia. *She speaks of the creature as though he is an honoured guest,* thought Talia.

"Yes, he has," Talia managed to say.

"Make friends with him, Mama. You and I are good with animals. Papa is not so good. Aherin always throws him off," Katie giggled. Talia almost giggled at the sheer absurdity of the thought. Talia wondered what Aiden would think of his daughter's suggestion.

"I will surely try, my love. I hope the dragon needs a new friend," Talia told her little girl as she gave her a tight hug and another kiss.

When it was time to part ways with Aiden, the anguish washed over her once more. There was so much more she wanted to say to him, but if she did, he would never let her go. The kiss they shared was different from the one she had given Katie. It was filled with love, hope, and, although neither of them said it, the sorrow of parting. Talia tried to capture their moment together for eternity, the love and sadness in Aiden's usually happy eyes, his grin, the warmth of his embrace, and his strength. She could taste salt on his lips. He was crying; she wanted to cry too. In fact, she wanted to bawl loudly, to scream and shout in protest. Fate had cruelly taken her parents and brother away from her, and now it was her husband and her daughter she was leaving behind. Tearing herself from her prince, she ran to Aherin and galloped out into the maze.

Aiden had never felt so helpless and adrift in his life. What had Talia been trying to say to him? It sounded awfully like a final parting. His mind was in turmoil trying to make sense of her words while his eyes remained riveted on the horse and rider slowly disappearing in the distance.

Aiden didn't see the tiny figure run out into the maze trying to follow Talia. Talia's outer façade of confidence and calmness had not fooled Katie. She sensed that her mother was in danger and she meant to do all she could to help. She had helped in the garden when they were attacked. She would do it again.

CHAPTER XXII

Father, you showed great kindness without expecting anything in return.
But good deeds have a way of returning to the giver.
Talia

JAESDAN—NABIA

NABIA LOOKED AT HER CHILDREN, Micha and Lina, gadding about the place. The two of them were brats. Adil was a good father but he spoiled them rotten. Usually, she would try to rein them in, but today her mind was on her old friends for some reason. Michael and Talia were in her thoughts. *Where are you?* she wondered.

When Caitlin and Joshua disappeared, Adil, Hachim, Beni and Mehdi went looking for them. Nabia visited Aberevon once too. Talia's fortitude, her grace under pressure and her determination to provide a stable and warm home for Michael won Nabia's heart. She was in a quandary about whether she should use the medallion or not. Nabia recalled how Caitlin had been extremely explicit in her instructions. *The medallion is to be used only if and when Michael is in trouble.* Michael was desolate and upset, but he was safe.

Michael was clueless as to the reason for Caitlin's disappearance. Nabia's loyalty lay first with Michael, but she had made Caitlin a promise and she meant to honour it.

Nabia's reluctance also stemmed from her rather traditional and superstitious early childhood days before she was orphaned. She had finally let her wariness of the supernatural gain the upper hand and had decided against calling Caitlin's sister, Ava.

Nabia had hidden the existence of the medallion from a distraught Michael, all the while unsure if she had made the right decision.

Nabia and Adil moved to another town for some years. The others looked out for Talia for a while, but Nabia lost touch with her. When they returned to Jaesdan many years later, it was to the news that four years after Caitlin and Joshua, Michael and Talia had also vanished from Aberevon. It was now many years since they were gone. The others had tried to find them, but without Adil's capable guidance and Nabia's soothing words, their efforts had gradually fizzled out.

Nabia was distraught. She became lost in our own world and felt she had let Caitlin down. But she was scared of magic. Before she lost her family, she had been taught to fear those who knew magic, and despite Caitlin's reassurances, it seemed the past still held its sway over her. Enough was enough. It was time to call for help. She hoped she wasn't too late. She went to her room and took out the tiny bronze scarab box in which she had kept the medallion hidden all these years. *Do something, Nabia. You have already waited too long. They are all gone now.*

Ommah Sahira! I forgot my duty to your family for a while. I hope I am doing the right thing now.

Caitlin had told her that if a day came when she felt that their baba was in trouble, she should use the medallion to call her sister. Ava would help her. All she had to do was clasp the medallion tightly in her palm until it grew very hot. *Would it still work after all these years?*

Nabia took the medallion in her hands and held on as tightly as she could, thinking of Michael, Caitlin and their children.

CHAPTER XXIII

Was my world any less magical because it was devoid of magic? I don't think so. Would I have been any less scared to face Damien if I had full control of my powers? Probably. But we must work with what we have. The goal was still the same—defeat Damien and win my freedom from his unwelcome attention, but the path would be as a mortal, not a powerful sorceress.
Talia

THE FACE-OFF—TALIA AND DAMIEN

AHERIN GALLOPED TOWARDS THE MAZE. The dragon had already set it on fire. If there were further onslaughts like this, the maze would not last long.

Seeing the approaching dragon, Talia was struck by a horrified sense of fascination. She had never seen such a magnificent creature before. As the dragon flew towards her, he was graceful despite his massive bulk.

As the fire was rapidly spreading through the maze, its light enveloped the dragon in a fiery blend of shimmering red, green and blue, giving him a mystical quality. However, his muscular limbs bore very real and sharp talons, warning Talia that this was no dream. His large nostrils were still smoking from the aftermath of all the fires set. A pair of dazzling black horns resplendent on his head made her feel that she had just come face to face with the very incarnation of the devil himself. She remembered how Jesse had called Aherin a devil. What would he say about the dragon? What captured her attention and almost hypnotized her were the hooded blue eyes of the dragon burning bright like blue flames, alert and watchful. They seemed to hold untold secrets, anger and even pain.

Talia wanted to run but she could not. It was now or all would be lost. She would lose the opportunity for vengeance and to save her family.

When Talia was finally able to look beyond the dragon, she spotted the man who had taken everything from her. As expected, Damien was astride the dragon. All these years Talia had feared him and built him up to terrifying proportions in her mind, but here he was, finally, a toy figure propped up to look like a warrior. His battle finery did nothing to hide his watery and pale persona or his weak chin and his shifty eyes. There was a time when he had frightened her more than the dragon, but now she saw him for what he truly was—a faint-hearted and craven king.

Aherin and Talia were so still that one would not blame the dragon if he mistook them for a sculpture. He was close now that all she had to do was stand in the stirrup and lift her hand, then she could touch the dragon. It may have been a good opportunity to push her sword into his soft underbelly, but she didn't.

The Dragon raised his head elegantly and let out such an outrageously loud cry that Talia thought her head would burst. At the same time, he brought one forelimb dangerously close to her. One swipe and she would be knocked aside with broken bones. Was the ground beneath her trembling, or was she? Talia willed herself to remain still, because calmness was her only defence in the face of something so majestic and powerful.

Closing her eyes, Talia thought about Joshua and Katie, the defenceless ones. She was doing this for them. It was some time before she realized that the cries of the dragon had given way to only the sound of the flickering flames licking at everything within their grasp.

Hovering in the air above her, the dragon caught sight of Talia and fell silent. He stared at the young woman below. He knew her. *How?* She looked a lot like the sorceress from the dungeon—a petite, waif-like creature but with nerves of steel.

Unaware of the dragon's thoughts, Talia thought it was time to end the charade. She had to put the freak show that was King Damien in his rightful place. She started galloping deep into the maze. Damien seemed to think she was running away from him and gave an angry shout.

"You think you can hide from my dragon in a paltry maze that I've already set on fire? I will soon burn it to the ground!" King Damien declared from the safety of the dragon's back.

Talia ignored him. When she was deeper within the maze, she stopped.

As the dragon again appeared in the air above, Damien jumped off. "At last!" he shouted. "You have lead me on a merry dance all these years. You let others take the fall on your behalf. First your mother and then your brother, not to mention all those girls who died in your place. "Who are you going to sacrifice to save your-self now?" he added derisively.

When it seemed that his taunts were having no effect on Talia, Damien brought out his most callous weapon yet. "Your poor father also paid the price for your cowardice. We caught him as soon as you ran away. He withstood the torture for many years. I think he was waiting for the day he would see you again, but when I showed him what had happened to your brother and told him what I was going to do to you, his heart gave out," Damien ground out cruelly.

Talia felt dazed, bereft. Her was father lost too. Was Damien intentionally trying to goad her with his lies, or was her father really dead? If it was a ploy to distract her, it seemed to be working. How could it not? With great effort, she managed to pull herself together. Now was not the time to grieve. To Damien, she was the prey and he the predator. He played to win, but now so must she. Rather than dwelling on the past, she must focus on all she had to protect in her present. If she gave in to her sorrow, he would win again.

Their positions must be reversed before Damien could make his move. He was watching her like a hawk as if expecting Talia to dismount and try to attack him. He hoped to draw her out, but Talia knew better. She had almost fooled him once in the past —not again.

Talia was staring intently at the dragon, which stared back. If the dragon took it in its head to attack her first, before she made her move, she would have to be in a position to escape. Dodging him on foot would make things much tougher, so she intended to stay on Aherin.

As Damien kept up his taunts, the dragon became more and more restless. He was a large dragon, a fearsome one, but standing behind King Damien, his antics looked almost playful. Talia wondered if her eyes were playing tricks on her. She wasn't too sure but it seemed like the dragon had his head cocked to one side and was staring at her.

As though reading her mind, the skittish dragon's brilliant blue eyes fixed themselves first on her and then on Aherin. He seemed to decide that the horse looked like a good creature to chase. With a loud roar, the dragon shot a blaze of fire towards an unsuspecting Aherin's hooves. The startled horse did not wait for

Talia's command. Rightly interpreting the dragon's action as a challenge, he started galloping like the wind with the dragon right at his tail. As Talia and Aherin raced ahead with the dragon zooming in behind them, Damien was left looking stupefied by the sudden turn in events. If the dragon killed Talia, all would be lost for him. "Don't kill her; she is mine. Come back here," he yelled at the dragon over the din of the crackling fire, but he was already long gone.

"Don't you dare kill my dragon," Damien screamed at Talia, who was even further away than the dragon. She obviously didn't hear his angry shout. Damien remained standing in the middle of the maze, transfixed by the sudden chaos erupting in front of him.

Meanwhile, Talia could almost feel the fire scorch her armour. Time held no meaning as woman and horse tried to outrun the dragon. Fear was driving Aherin. The Arabian looked like he was almost flying through the air, but he seemed unable to shake off the dragon tailing them. Turning a corner, the lumbering and gigantic creature temporarily dropped out of sight, allowing Talia to breathe a sigh of relief. She was back near the centre of the maze now. It was time to face her dragon. Darkness had almost fallen, but while the flames engulfed the entire maze, increasing the danger, they also improved Talia's visibility.

After Aherin came to a halt, Talia dismounted, readying her crossbow and lance. Was she going to have to kill the dragon? What alternative did she have?

It was time to let Aherin go. Whispering, "Go, Aherin. Go to Katie," Talia stepped back knowing the mere mention of Katie's name would send Aherin to her. It was only in Katie's presence that the wild Arabian took on the docility of a pony, abandoning the rather aggressive side of his personality, which victims like Jesse and Aiden had discovered in the past, much to their own woe.

Aherin would head back to Katie, of that Talia was sure, but instead of moving to the exit of the maze, she saw her faithful horse doubling back. Aherin had never disobeyed her before. Instead of the palace, why was he heading towards Damien? The only logical explanation terrified her. "No, Katie. Not you too. I cannot lose you too!" Talia screamed. She almost started running back to Damien but then she stilled her petrified heart. Damien believed Katie was a sorceress too, so she would be safe for now. He would not kill anyone he had use for. If Katie, and in fact all of them, were to survive, Talia had to stop the dragon from returning to his master. There was so much at stake that she did not have the luxury of making a single mistake. She would deal with the dragon first, and then take care of Damien.

CHAPTER XXIV

Dragon, what does it feel like to realize you were right all along? In your heart, you felt conflict between what you were deep inside and what you were supposed to be. Now you know why.
Talia

THE HEART OF A DRAGON

WHERE HAD that horse vanished to? The dragon had to find the one his master called Talia. He did not want to kill her or terrify her. He just wanted to see her again. Happiness was an emotion alien to him, but it had been bubbling to the surface from deep within as soon as he had seen her.

Why?

With startling clarity, the dragon knew he could never hurt the princess of Syrolt even if his master commanded him to do so. It was a dictate he would be forced to ignore.

He would not kill his own sister—his precious Talia.

The thick, voluminous curtain that choked his memories had started lifting from the moment he set his eyes on Talia. The haze that veiled his recollections began to fade away. She was not just Talia, Princess of Syrolt, or the sorceress hunted by King Damien. She was also his precious older sister

Talia was acting like a stranger. She looked at Joshua with awe and fear instead of love. She believed that Joshua, the apple of her eye, was dead. All she saw was King Damien's powerful fire-breathing dragon, a destroyer and a predator. No wonder she looked at him with such distaste.

How had it come to be that Talia was terrified of him?

THE WINDOW to the past opened, bringing memories that he, Joshua, had chosen to hide from for so long: His mother pleading and crying; King Damien whipping him with a long, sharp and evil looking lash. He was cowering in the corner and screaming in pain. Even worse than the beatings were the nights in the dungeon when he was separated from his mother. He would call out Talia's name, afraid of the monsters in the dark. She never heard him. How could she? But he would still call her, using her name as a talisman against the dark until morning came.

His final memory, his last day in his old body—*Joshua's body*—he lay broken and battered at his mother's feet. The guards who attacked him had backed away, scared of the angry and terrified sorceress and her dying son. Her screams of protest and then sobs of anguish tore at his heart. He was small and weak, only nine years old, but in his mind's eye, he saw himself as a *brave knight*. He had only wanted to stop Garcia from hurting his mother, but by rushing in, he'd made things worse.

As he lay dying, his mother's anguish was unbearable. His eyes, blue as the ocean and just as beautiful as his mother's, closed. It became too much of a struggle to keep them open. He looked at his mother and tried his best to smile. *Brave until the end; that's what he would be.* He didn't want her to cry anymore.

Uncontrollable tears of anguish and regret rolled down Caitlin's cheeks. "I don't care what the Wraith told me, Joshua; I have to try to save you."

Ignoring the cries from the guards, for they dared not come near her, she put one hand on his forehead and the other on his almost shattered chest and began whispering to him. At first, nothing happened. Then the air around them seemed to spin and swirl. It felt like he was caught right in the middle of it. Then the real torment started.

Joshua barely felt the earlier pain because his mind had gone numb and his imagination had taken over. He saw himself happy and exhilarated, basking in the warmth of his family. He saw his sister's arms open in a welcoming embrace. He knew that once he reached her, the twinges of pain he felt would soon go away. It would be over.

But it seemed fate had decreed otherwise.

Caitlin's spell only intensified the pain manifold. Joshua's dream shattered and his mind became trapped in a cycle of torture from which there was no escape. His insides were pulled in all directions and his skin had felt like it was tearing at the seams. It went on and on until he slept from the sheer combination of agony and fatigue.

When Joshua finally awoke, Caitlin was still standing in front of him, her eyes wide with terror and sorrow, but at that moment, she was a stranger to him.

The broken, lifeless body Caitlin cradled in her arms once belonged to him when he was Joshua; *he knew that now.* He looked at the body in her arms, his own empty shell, and failed to recognise himself or even his own mother.

Caitlin had ignored the dire warnings of her Elders and succeeded in saving his life, but not in the way she had hoped.

Caitlin had protected Joshua's soul but his mortal body rejected her magic. His soul, the essence of everything that was Joshua, had been freed of his broken body and was now encased in the strong and mighty form of a supernatural—a dragon.

Joshua's soul had entered the dragon that Caitlin had summoned from Htrae. It was imprisoned in the dragon.

CHAPTER XXV

Ah, what joy when the past comes full circle and meets the present.
Talia

~

 REUNION

JOSHUA FINALLY FOUND HIS SISTER, or rather he found her waiting for him.

The Talia who stood before him was the same yet different. She still had the beauty of their mother but she also had the determination of their father too.

Today she was a Heichi warrior. Her blue locks were free and flowing. It was a declaration of her identity. *I am not hiding anymore*, she seemed to be saying. Her eyes, so much like his own, were fiery and burning with an intensity that reflected anger and revenge. But contrary to a warrior's battle readiness, her weapons lay discarded in a pile to the side. *What do you want?* he wanted to ask. *To talk or to fight?*

Talia wore a thoughtful expression on her face. Joshua had seen this expression before. It meant she wanted to talk. The dragon in him was taken aback. Aiming a stake at his heart would have been a lot easier than throwing herself at his mercy. The most significant hallmark of any friendship is trust. By standing there weaponless without a single soldier in sight, she had done something that King Damien never had. She expressed faith in the dragon's discernment and empathy. Talia was going to try to win over the dragon. She seemed determined to attempt what no one had done before—appeal to the better instincts of a dragon. Dragons very rarely accepted humans of their own free will. Did she not know that? What if he were to kill her?

The dragon waited. She would say her piece eventually, and she did but without saying a word. She reached out directly to him through her thoughts just like he suspected their mother could. *"I do not want to kill you. Enough innocent lives have been lost. Don't stand in my way. Don't protect Damien. Win your freedom and I will win my vengeance and protect my family,"* she pleaded.

Joshua fixed his blue eyes on Talia in a hypnotic stare. He could see right into her heart, the compassion, love, and courage. She was just the same—his beloved sister with a deep desire to protect the family she has today and to avenge the ones she thought she had lost. No self-serving obsession like King Damien. Her soul had a golden aura. It was magical and filled with the most beautiful thing in the world—love.

How could he make her look into his heart? *Don't you know me, Talia?* he wanted to ask. If only he could give her a great big hug to make up for the loss of the past years of anguish. Then he remembered.

Before her amazed eyes, Talia saw the massive dragon, who was looking very uncomfortable in the relative tight fit of the maze, slowly start to spin. He wasn't encircling her, trying to block her escape or attack. His moves were far from aggressive. She did not know how to react to such puzzling behaviour. He was turning around in a small circle while standing in the same place. Then he stopped and looked at her. Was he expecting some response? What? This was unexpected.

Talia had counted on being targeted and attacked. Not this. This was surely abnormal behaviour for a dragon. When all she did was stare at him open mouthed, he shook his gigantic head from side to side as if in exasperation, and then he repeated the same thing again. He went on and on. She could not take it anymore. "You are going to get dizzy," she said, when in fact she was the one feeling light headed, but the dragon just shook his head and went on with his task.

Again and again he kept turning around in circles.

As Talia watched, the scene in front of her faded; the dragon was gone and time turned back for her. She saw Joshua twisting and spiralling, going around and around, laughing, giggling but refusing to stop until she hugged him. It could not be. She stared and stared at the dragon.

What was it that Damien had said? *I showed him what happened to your brother and told him what I was going to do to you. His heart gave out.*

Was it possible that she hadn't lost Joshua after all?

Talia had nothing to lose. At the most, the dragon would set her on fire, but if he wanted to kill her, he could have done so by now. She would not be taking a greater risk than she already was just by standing in his presence.

Talia ran towards the circling dragon. Seeing her so close, he faltered, almost as if he was scared too. Taking a deep breath, hoping she wasn't making the greatest mistake of her life, she stepped forward gingerly and almost deferentially ran her hands over his scales. They were neither sharp nor rough like she had imagined but as smooth as pebbles polished by the flowing waters of a river.

Talia spread her arms as wide as she could and gave the dragon a great big hug. She made a gigantic assumption but she had nothing to lose. She put all her love and hope into the embrace, casting her past disappointments away.

Had it started raining? Water was dripping on her head. It meant she was still alive. All her limbs were intact. Stepping back, she craned her neck upwards to look at the dragon.

The dragon was standing still, his head bowed. It wasn't rain that she had felt but his tears.

"Joshua?" she asked, cautiously.

The dragon looked at her, his eyes shining. He vigorously nodded. She finally recognized him. "Oh, Joshua, how did this happen to you? Don't worry; I will make it all right," she said, planting a kiss on his salty and scaly cheek. "I will get you your body back; I promise." Then her smile turned into a distressed frown. "You have a niece, Joshua. She is six and she is beautiful. Damien has her and he is waiting for me."

Knowing that another family member was in the clutches of King Damien riled Joshua like nothing else could. This had to end permanently. King Damien had to be stopped. His actions had taken away some of the sweetness of his reunion with Talia, but there would be time enough to celebrate later. It was time to face King Damien. He must get Talia there quickly. Her mount was nowhere in sight.

Joshua gave a mighty purr and bent his forelegs. He then flattened his long and powerful tail to the ground, allowing Talia to climb onto his back. Joshua waited a beat, but the bond between them was as seamless as ever. Talia understood. As soon as she climbed onto his back, ensuring her grip around his neck was firm, he lifted his massive body off the ground, tail arched as straight as an arrow, wings unfurled to full length like the twin masts of a large ship.

The dragon glided into the air as graceful as a swan and headed towards King Damien.

CHAPTER XXVI

The thing about fear is that it is always greater when it lives in your heart. Bring it out in the open and sometimes it has no choice but to be gone.
The thing about a weapon you create to use against others is that sometimes it turns right back on you.
Talia

THE MORTAL KING

THE DRAGON SET Talia down a few feet away from Damien with a tenderness that belied his size. The king stood triumphantly holding Katie against his chest, her feet dangling helplessly in the air. An unsheathed sword lovingly grazed Katie's neck, the threat against the child implicit.

Damien's cocky expression turned stormy when he saw Talia's ride. He shook Katie in anger. That wretched dragon was always trying to befriend humans even though he had lost his own humanity. The poisonous looks he directed towards the dragon would have usually been enough to make the dragon shiver in fear, but not this time. The little girl's cries enraged him. When he looked at Katie, he saw a little Talia in Damien's cruel grip.

Damien had successfully used the threat of violence to coerce Joshua in the past, but no more. He had an identity. He wasn't a dragon. He never had been. He was Joshua, brother of Talia and son of Michael and Caitlin, and that should count for something even if he was trapped in the body of a dragon.

Finding the dragon impervious to his taunting looks, Damien turned on Talia instead. "Took your time, didn't you? Almost had a change of heart about your daughter's worth now that you've managed to charm my dragon?"

"Never," said Talia. "Nothing is more important to me than family."

"I am here now, Katie. You've been a brave girl and I am proud of you," Talia said to her.

"You aren't angry with me for following you?" Katie asked. Katie's shouting and howling had driven Damien crazy, but seeing Talia, she had quietened down considerably with only the occasional hiccup tempering a sudden sob.

"Hmm, only a little," said Talia, forcing laughter into her voice. Katie finally stopped sobbing altogether and gave a small smile. Damien sighed in relief when the racket died down but the way the mother and daughter were carrying on as though he wasn't even there was too much. To add to his woes, his dragon seemed to have switched sides. He wished he had his whip with him. That would have quickly got the dragon back in control.

"You managed to charm my dragon like you did me the first time we met," commented Damien in a chatty voice, something else clearly simmering beneath the surface. "Does he remind you of someone you used to know?" he asked in jeering voice.

Talia could no longer maintain the mask of ignorance. "You

knew!" she spat out. "You knew and you still forced him to kill for you? He was just a child. How could you? There has to be a limit to your depravity."

"Does your brother still look like a child? I am not the one who turned him into a dragon, am I?" Damien retorted mildly. "It was your mother. If he wasn't going to serve me, I would have got rid of him. You should thank me for keeping him alive even though he is a sign of your mother's betrayal," Damien told Talia. "Aren't you disgusted by what he has become?" Grasping the struggling Katie tighter, Damien began laughing. "Your father was disgusted. He was so determined to learn the truth. I just helped him along, but instead of being happy to see your brother, he collapsed and died."

The dragon roared in anger again, only succeeding in inciting the king to laugh louder.

"You are a terrible person," Talia said. "You will be punished for what you have done. You have had your fun. Let her go now," Talia insisted as she took a step closer.

"Of course not. This little charmer is my guarantee that you will do as I say. Come here," he commanded.

"Katie is a child. What power do you think she will give you? If a single hair on her head is harmed, I will not be of any use to you," threatened Talia.

Recalling how Joshua had put a spoke in his plans, the king hesitated. He knew she wasn't lying. *Like mother, like daughter,* he whispered to himself. Caitlin had been ready to do anything to save Joshua, and Talia would do the same for Katie. These sorceresses were mothers before anything else. *What a waste of power.*

"I will come back to Aberevon with you, but you need to let her go and give me Joshua back," Talia promised.

"Katie is not going anywhere. Besides, I can't give you your brother back. The ghosts who came for your mother also took away his body. Even with magic, how do you plan to change this creature back into a boy without his body?" Damien snorted derisively, pointing at the dragon.

Talia wanted to kill Damien right then but she knew that he spoke the truth. This was the Wraith her father had told her about, the ones who had doomed her mother's life. She would get Joshua back, but first they had to free Katie. The lance would have been perfect, but all she had now was the sword.

From the rear side of the maze, Aiden suddenly appeared. He did not seem to have any weapons on him. He must have run after Katie when he realized she was missing. Talia saw him but did not react. His appearance gave her the hope that the situation could yet be retrieved. She deliberately turned her focus back to the belligerent king to distract him from any noise Aiden might accidentally make.

Katie saw Aiden and was about to call out to him, so Talia shouted, "Katie, fall forward! Now!" For a moment, neither Katie nor Damien reacted. Then, for once in her life, instead of arguing back, the little girl did as she was told. She almost slipped out of Damien's grasp, surprising him, but he did not let go. Damien, engaged and absorbed in holding on to Katie, did not see Aiden. Aiden shoved the king aside, grabbing hold of the little girl at the same time. Eager to be of help, Talia rushed to them. Damien threw her to the ground and pointed his sword at her.

"Let us see how immortal you are. Will you survive my sword plunging into your heart? If I can't have you, no one can."

A familiar voice spoke in Talia's head. It was Joshua reaching out to her. *Do you remember the furnace and how father chewed you up for going near it?* Before Talia could react, the voice shouted, *"Move! Now! It is furnace time again."*

Talia ducked out of the way without a second thought. If Katie could follow orders blindly, so could she.

Once, a long time ago, with the absurd curiosity that only children possess, she had gone closer to a huge furnace than she should have. The heat had exploded all around her, torrid, blistering, red-hot and scorching. Luckily, her father had pulled her away just in time, but the yelling she'd received from him had not been any less fiery. Joshua had been witness. He was the one who had consoled her, holding her tight in his little arms.

As she watched, a blast of fire walled Damien in. The warmth of the furnace had been positively chilly compared to the scorching heat emitting from her brother. Stunned, she watched as Damien's deathly prison of flames encircled him until his struggling figure was no longer visible. He literally vanished from sight having been burned to ashes just like his victims

Death by the very dragon he used as a weapon to kill countless of innocents. Damien's own instrument of death had turned on him. Wasn't this justice and a fitting retribution?

Another peril had arisen in the maze. Damien was dead but the dragon's fiery flames continued unabated. Joshua was exercising his own free will for the first time in his prevailing avatar, seeking vengeance for all the infractions that Damien had heaped on him and their family.

Damien had channelled the strength of the dragon for his own ends, and at the same time, manipulated and exploited Joshua's weaknesses as a child. Dragon he might have been in power, but in reality, Joshua was driven by the feelings, fears and anxieties of a nine-year-old boy. The fire raining down represented the angst, pain and resentment Joshua had bottled up inside against Damien.

Talia knew her brother needed an outlet to release his anger. Joshua had finally built up the courage to face the man who had destroyed him. He was hurting, but if he didn't stop, her husband and daughter would also be killed by the dragon's fire.

"It's over, Joshua, STOP!" Talia shouted. But Joshua either couldn't hear her over the din, or had chosen to ignore her. She skirted the path of his fiery flames and made her way to him as fast as she could.

Aiden and Katie watched, their expressions a mixture of awe and terror as Talia embraced the predatory looking dragon as though he were Aherin or a harmless palace pet. They didn't know the dragon was Talia's little brother and wouldn't harm her for anything in the world.

The flames sprouting from the dragon's mouth gradually subsided. They faded away as Talia's wordless embrace offered unconditional understanding and support to her beloved brother. He would never be alone again. He was where he belonged. With his family.

Tears of relief flooded Talia's eyes, but she quickly wiped them away with the back of her hand when she spotted a pale, shimmering, but very familiar figure at the periphery of her vision. "Mama?" she whispered in surprise.

CHAPTER XXVII

What happens when the past and the present collide? Which do you choose: A bright future filled with happiness at the cost of the sacrifices and pain of loved ones in the past? Or do you right the wrong?
Talia

A LIFE FOR A LIFE —TALIA

TALIA STARED at the ethereal and translucent lady standing before her—*Caitlin, her mother*. To Talia, it appeared as though her mother had just stepped out from a painting, for in appearance, she was as vivid as a muse created by the brush strokes of a master, but there was a lustre and brightness lacking in her eyes. *Is she real, a ghost like the Wraith, or just a figment of my imagination?*

"None of those," said Caitlin as though reading Talia's mind. "As a punishment for misusing the powers of the Heichi, I have been banished to the realm of the spirits, the great beyond, the unknown, but I am the only one who still retains my human form. I feel hunger, thirst, pain, sorrow and joy, but my prison is an eternal one. I have returned to you here on Earth just this one time."

"Oh, no, Mama!" sobbed Talia. Talia remembered and recognized every distinctive feature of her mother's face. There were lines where earlier there had been none. Despite her mother's ageing, it was as if Talia was but a child again, holding Caitlin's hand and staring adoringly at her.

There was so much she wanted to say to her mother but she didn't even know where to begin. The words and emotions had been contained inside her for so long. *Why did you run away?* she wanted to ask. *Father was in pieces without you and Joshua.* But all she said was, "Mama, you're alive! You came back. I missed you so much."

"And it seems that I have missed out on so much that has happened in your life," Caitlin said, casting a lingering glance towards Aiden and Katie through the murky haze. "All grown up with a family of your own. When I left, you were only twelve, a little girl."

Talia nodded, "Yes, mother. I never thought I would have a family again, but here they are. Aiden, my husband, and my daughter, Katie and that is Jo—"

"He is so handsome and she is beautiful. So much like you when you were a child," Caitlin interrupted her wistfully.

But news of Joshua couldn't be avoided any longer. *Does mother know?* "Do you know that Joshua..." asked Talia sounding worried. How would Caitlin react?

"Joshua is a dragon," Caitlin completed for her. "I know. That is the reason I am here; his time on Earth is done. It is time for him to leave" she said, her voice laced with sorrow. "I am so glad I also got a chance to see you one last time to say goodbye. I didn't earlier... I just left. I couldn't say goodbye, otherwise I would have not been able to leave."

It had been useless to hope her mother had returned to them, but as her hope for her mother's return faded, she realized what Caitlin had whispered.

What did mean by his time on Earth is done? Talia wondered.

Despite the searing heat around them, the dragon seemed to be shivering. "Joshua, why are you afraid?" Talia asked. "It's only Mama." But the dragon seemed to sense what Talia couldn't, until finally she felt it too. An unexplained coldness was spreading around them. She could almost feel her own breath grow icy. "What is it, Joshua? What is happening?" she asked.

"They are coming," said Caitlin, sounding scared too. "The Wraith."

"Why?" asked Talia. "Don't they come only when they have to guide a spirit into the Ether World? Damien wasn't a supernatural, so why are they here?"

"For Joshua," said Caitlin in a voice laden with sorrow. "The dragon as we see him is an aberration, and such anomalies are not allowed to live on either Htrae, the magical realm of the supernaturals, or Earth. It would create an imbalance between clans. It already has, hence the Wraith are here to restore order. They wanted to take him the very day my magic went wrong, but I forced them to give Joshua some more time on Earth, even if trapped in the dragon's body. Their condition was that the day Joshua got his revenge would be his last," Caitlin explained.

"And Damien's death gave him his revenge," finished Talia, understanding dawning.

Caitlin nodded and continued. "I wanted to save him but I have failed again. I had nothing more to offer them. I am here because I know he will be afraid. I will not abandon him this time. I have let him down too often."

"Take Joshua away? No, no, it can't be. It's not fair. He deserves his life back," cried Talia. This couldn't be happening. She had just found her brother yet here was her mother telling her he had to leave again and there was nothing she could do. She wouldn't stand by this time around and be a hapless victim to her brother being separated from her, but the sadness in Caitlin's eyes said it all. The Wraith never returned empty handed. They already had Caitlin; now they were coming for Joshua.

As Talia racked her head for a solution, pale, ghostly figures surrounded her, Caitlin and Joshua. Talia neither feared nor venerated the Wraith, the revered spirits of the Heichi sorceresses who watched over the supernaturals rather than walking away into the light of the unknown or the Ether World. For her family, they had always been mere forecasters of doom. They had destroyed her mother's life and consequently their entire family's chance at happiness. She wouldn't let them have the same power over her too.

Talia glanced at Joshua. *Deep inside, he is still a child*, a startled Talia realized. He looked like a dragon, he could do all a dragon could, but in his heart and soul, he was her baby brother. His strangled cries made Talia realize that Joshua knew they had come for him. He had been through so much. Would his torture and misfortune never end? She had lost him twice already. She couldn't let this happen for a third time, no matter what the cost.

As Talia watched, another shiver ran down the entire length of the mighty dragon and the Wraith whispered restlessly. They were eager to be gone.

Caitlin had nothing to offer the Wraith, but Talia realized she did. She had something of value the Wraith couldn't refuse. She fell to her knees before the spirits, and, joining her hands, she pleaded, "Make my brother whole again. It is time for him to live the life he was meant to. Allow him to grow into the wonderful man he can be. Give him the childhood that was snatched away from him before his time. In return, I offer you this. Instead of him, take me," said Talia. "A life for a life."

There was silence all around. Nothing could be heard but the whispers of the Wraith. When it seemed like hours had passed but, in fact, it was only minutes, the spirits extended their hands towards her. *"Come,"* they said. "You will join your mother in her prison."

Hearing these words, Talia knew the deal was sealed. They accepted her offer. She was so intent on their decision that she didn't hear Caitlin's exclamation of shock and Aiden's cry of protest. Katie and Aiden were locked outside the circle the Wraith had created, but they had heard her plea.

Aiden was shattered. *How could she?* "No, Talia, no. Please don't go," he pleaded. Still carrying Katie, he ran towards Talia. "We will find a way to keep both of you," he said, tears flowing freely now. But both Caitlin and Talia knew it was too late. The bargain had already been made with the spirits. Talia wouldn't be allowed to back out now.

The circle of ghostly figures seemed to be coming closer. One smaller figure broke away from the circle, his body made whole again by magic. He ran forward straight into the dragon, merging with the beast. The dragon gave a cry of pain. His large body began to shake and quiver. The separation of Joshua's soul from the dragon had started. Very soon, Joshua would no longer need the dragon, his host, for he would have his own body back again.

This also meant that it was time for Talia to go.

"Don't cross their circle," Talia shouted out to Aiden. She could see the desperation in his eyes. Fearful of the harm that could come to him and Katie, she begged, "If you love me, stay back." Her voice filled with both regret and determination, she said, "My parents and brother sacrificed a lot for me to have this life with you. Joshua's childhood was taken away from him so cruelly. I have to do what I can to give him a chance at life. I know I am asking a lot from you, but if I don't do this, I can never be whole again. A part of me will die with him. Please allow me to save him. Please be there for him," said Talia, her cheeks damp with tears. Aiden shook his head in denial and defeat. His dilemma was great. He couldn't leave Katie alone, neither could he cross the circle with her. It would be too dangerous. What if the Wraith decided to take her away too? He had to save Talia? He couldn't live without her.

Meanwhile, Talia turned to Katie. "Katie, my love, Mama has to go away, but you have a new brother, Joshua, who will be coming to live with you. He is only a few years older than you, so you will now have lots of company. You must be brave and remember I love you very much," sobbed Talia.

"I want a brother, Mama, but please don't go. We need you too," pleaded Katie, but it was too late.

The Wraith stared at Talia. "I won't go back on my word," she said. Her voice quivered as she turned to Caitlin. "Mama, help me be brave." Caitlin immediately held out her hand to her daughter as she too cast one last loving look towards Joshua.

From the beginning, both of them would have given anything to protect Joshua. Caitlin had bought him time on Earth by going against her own clan, and now Talia was going to save him from the Wraith. Their only regret was for the loved ones she would never see again.

The spirits kept their word. Joshua would soon be whole and human again. He must never know Talia had sacrificed herself for him. As for the dragon, would it be able to return to Htrae, to its old life? Hopefully it would be happy, the conflict between soul and nature finally over. It had sheltered Joshua for so long and lent him its strength when he needed it the most. It deserved a chance at happiness too.

Talia turned towards Aiden and Katie for one last look. "Goodbye, Aiden, my love. Take care of the children. I will always treasure the memories we built together...wherever I may be." Her fingers briefly linked with Aiden's through the circle of the Wraith, and then she brushed Katie's soft cheek.

∼

THE WRAITH APPEARED to be little more than wisps of smoke as they began to depart as quietly as they had come. All that remained behind was the fulfilment of their vow in the form of a boy only a couple of years older than Katie with Talia's eyes.

The mighty dragon gave one last roar of farewell and flew away. Higher and higher it went. Joshua stared at the retreating dragon. His mind felt clear but strangely empty of the burden of memories humans tend to grasp at. He only remembered that he was called Joshua. Another name tugged at his consciousness; he knew it was important. How, he wasn't quite sure, but he knew that he had to hold on to it. His body felt drained and weary but free and exulted at the same time. Having no memory of the past, he couldn't understand the unexplained connection he felt with the gigantic creature he could see flying in the distance.

"Goodbye, my friend," said Joshua as the dragon became a distant speck in the sky. *Where am I? What is happening?* he wondered. *Maybe he knows something,* thought Joshua as he looked at Aiden standing in front of him. The rising temperature of the ruined maze had him scurrying straight to Aiden.

"Do you know who Talia is and where can I find her?" Joshua asked Aiden, panic filling his voice. Talia's name and his own were the only things he had to hold on to. Katie sensed the boy's confusion. She bent from her father's arms to clasp his hand. "Calm down," she said. "It is going to be okay. Talia is your friend but she had to leave. I will be your friend; father and I will look after you."

Seeing his confusion, Aiden quietly stepped ahead and enveloped him in one-armed hug. Seeing how forlorn and lost Joshua looked, Aiden added, "She isn't here, but I am, and I promise you I will get her back one day." Joshua's vulnerability reminded Aiden of Jesse in his younger days. No wonder Talia had been so fond of his nephew. She had always seen her beloved Joshua in him.

Katie whimpered, "I feel hot, very hot." Her words made Aiden conscious of the fire blazing around them, spreading through the maze at an alarming speed. He was responsible for the two children. He had to leave and get them to safety. One day he would get Talia back, but for now, Joshua and Katie came first.

Aherin was whinnying into the wind. Was it the heat, or did the Arabian also feel the loss of Talia's departure? As though hearing his name, the frightened horse galloped towards Aiden.

The flames were rising as though appealing to the heavens and trying to trap the motley group of victims in its embrace. Aiden lifted Joshua and Katie onto Aherin, and with one last glance behind, even though he knew Talia was no longer there, he mounted Aherin too. Sheltering the children within the circle of his arms, Aiden told them to hold on tight. They had to get out of the maze before the entire thing collapsed.

The fire or the smoke: which would get to them first? Hopefully neither.

"Jump, Aherin," said Aiden. Without needing another command, the usually temperamental horse started galloping towards the outer wall of the maze, leaving the last vestiges of the past behind. Despite the heat engulfing them, Aiden realized that this was the first time Aherin had obeyed him. It only served as a confirmation that his Talia was truly gone.

The smoke must have blinded and suffocated Aherin, but still the faithful mount continued moving swiftly towards the high walls of the maze. His hooves must have started blistering from the scorching heat on the ground, but his steady gallop gave no indication of it. With his passengers holding on for dear life, suddenly he was airborne and they were flying through the air and over the maze.

The soldiers rushed towards them. There was Andrea with Ellie by her side waiting to take a dazed Katie and Joshua from Aiden's arms.

"What are you doing here?" Aiden managed to ask, wondering if he was hallucinating. With so much supernatural power all around, he needed to confirm that the vision before him was indeed his own flesh and blood sister and not some phantom trying to steal the children away. The children were special and all he had left.

"Talia wrote asking us to come. She said you may need us," said Ellie simply.

"She said ask no questions but be there for Aiden, and that is just what we are going to do," said Andrea.

Joshua allowed himself to be enveloped in a warm hug by Andrea. He didn't know who she was but she seemed kind. With each child in the custody of one of the women, the party of rescuers and the rescued made their way back to the castle with tired feet and blackened faces. All except for Aiden, who found himself unable to leave.

Aiden stood watching the flames burning brightly. Had he lost Talia forever? No, he wouldn't allow that.

You wanted me to keep Katie and Joshua safe. They are. Damien is no longer a danger to them. Soon I will soon be riding out to find you. We are meant to be together. Guide me if you can. Aiden didn't know if Talia could hear him or not, but he knew that one day he would be reunited with her whatever the cost. The spirits had taken his very reason for living. He had to get her back.

As the wind whispered around him, Aiden was almost sure he still sensed Talia in the silence of the burning flames.

CHAPTER XXVIII

I never believed that this was possible. The two men I love—one who put his life on the line for me, and one who taught me how to live again—would meet and would have a common purpose: finding me.
Talia

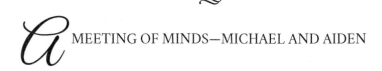

$\mathscr{A}$ MEETING OF MINDS—MICHAEL AND AIDEN

"YOU NEVER DID TELL me what happened with King Damien. Why did you collapse? What brought it on?" asked Luigi.

When Damien initially told Talia that seeing what happened to his son killed Michael, Talia had taken it to mean Damien was talking about her brother's death. Michael had indeed collapsed. Taking him for dead, Damien threw Michael's inert body and the badly starved and injured Luigi beyond the castle walls of Aberevon. The two men were then taken outside the castle gates and their bodies dumped in a nearby forest for the animals.

When Luigi stood before him, Damien said, "Do not claim that I did not reward you for your work. Despite your treachery, I am giving you the gift of your life. Go and be grateful."

Luigi couldn't believe he had survived King Damien's dungeon only to face death in a forest. He stared in shock at his friend's body, sorrow sweeping through him knowing that because of him, a family was in shambles. *Let the girl be safe,* was his prayer.

Damien didn't realize he was inadvertently setting not one but two men free.

As Luigi lay weeping over his friend's body, he felt Michael's shallow breathing. His friend still lived.

Luigi was quick to use his familiarity with ancient medical texts and traditional healing methods to bring Michael back from death's doorstep, nature providing him what he needed.

Before he regained consciousness, Michael lay suspended in a sort of vacuum as his body healed. Fire kept the animals at bay, and when Michael finally found himself well enough to make a short journey, they set off for a tiny hamlet on the other side of the forest. Close to Aberevon but yet forgotten by its stately occupants, it was the perfect sanctuary for the two men.

Both men had believed that only their tortured and dead bodies would leave the dungeon. It had taken some getting used to the miraculous fact that the both of them had made it out alive.

When Luigi asked Michael what had happened, Michael had a question for him in return. "The dragon down there with us, the one chained in a large cell of the dungeon, do you remember him?"

"Of course I do. Who could forget the rumbling and the roars emerging from its cell, especially at night? I didn't even know dragons existed. But if sorceresses can, I suppose dragons can too. But why do you ask?" said Luigi.

"That...the dragon...it was my lost boy, Joshua," stammered Michael.

"What do you mean? I thought Garcia killed your boy. He

boasted about it to me. How can a huge, monstrous dragon be your son? You are not making any sense at all, Michael. You saw your boy's body. Isn't that the reason you collapsed?" Luigi asked, fearful that Michael had caught a fever.

"I am not hallucinating, Luigi. I am telling you the truth. Damien took me to the dragon's cell. I thought he was going to feed me to it. He laughed and said he was saddled with a stupid dragon that refused to eat humans. He then asked me why I couldn't recognize my own son. I didn't understand at first, so he explained that Joshua had been dying and in order to save him, my wife had used magic, magic that was poison to our son. Imagine my little boy right in front of me hissing in anger, cowering in fear of Damien and totally unable to recognize me. Can you imagine what it felt like knowing he was alive but lost to me forever?" Michael said in anguish. "But that's not all," continued Michael. "If the shock of seeing Joshua like this was not enough, Damien told me he had found Talia and was going after her, and if she didn't do as he wanted, he was going to make the dragon kill her. The thought of my son killing my daughter…I couldn't bear it, Luigi. I couldn't breathe. I was terrified. Panic must have brought on the attack."

Luigi looked thoughtful. "So now what do we do? We can't rush in to save your daughter. We don't even know where she is. Hopefully she has been resourceful enough to save herself."

"It has been more than a year. My fear is that sometimes Talia is too resourceful. She always puts others before herself."

"Just like her father," commented Luigi. "First there is something else we may have to worry about. We will need to move from here soon. I fear there is someone out there looking for us. I've been so careful I can't understand how the king's men may have found us."

"Were they asking for you or me?" asked Michael sharply. "Damien thinks I am dead, so he would only be looking for you."

"I am pretty sure the men were asking about you. One was tall, well-built, dark haired with a generous beard. The other of medium height with fair hair and a moustache."

The beginning of a smile began to appear on Michael's face, confusing Luigi. "Resourceful as you are, you wouldn't have happened to catch their names, would you?" Michael asked, hope resonating in his voice.

"Adil and Beni," said Luigi. "Do you know them? Are they enemies of yours? They have been going around and asking for you. There is a third man with them but he has been very secretive about his identity and is rarely seen with them, but I am quite sure that they know him. Would be quite a coincidence for this little place to be suddenly beset with strangers. Luckily, no one has seen you except the physician, and he is unaware of your real name. I'm afraid they could be spies or hunters of the king."

Michael started laughing. "Those two boys are my children, my beloved children and my oldest friends. I don't know about the third man. Where are they? Let's find them and get them here," said Michael, explaining to Luigi all about his relationship with the children of Jaesdan.

THERE WERE plenty of tears and laughter at the reunion with between Michael and his children. The men, they could no longer be called boys, had almost given up and were headed home. A frantic Nabia had sent them to search for Michael. They had returned to Aberevon despite the danger, but fortunately, news of his supposed death was secret and so they had kept looking. They found someone else looking for Talia or anyone from her family.

It was time to confront the stranger. Michael looked at the tall man standing in front of him. He was almost the same height, if not taller. But it was his eyes that drew Michael's attention. They were filled with pain and sorrow, the exact kind that had dwelt in

Michael's own eyes when Caitlin and Joshua went missing. Before he could say a word, the man spoke.

"She really wanted us to meet. She thought we would get along. She thought you were dead. King Damien told her he killed you," he said.

"You are talking about my Talia," said Michael, hope springing in his eyes. "Who are you to her?"

"I am Aiden, Talia's husband and your son-in-law. I need your help, but first I have some good news for you. Your son..." said Aiden, "Joshua is alive."

"I know," said Michael sorrowfully. "I have seen him. He is Joshua but he is not exactly Joshua, is he? He is a dragon."

"No, that's what I am trying to tell you. He is Joshua, the child you lost, the exact same child. He is with my sister and my daughter, your granddaughter, right now. He is safe. Damien is no more. Joshua, as the dragon, killed him."

Michael gave Aiden an incredulous look but only saw sincerity in the young man's expression. When he'd seen the massive dragon straining against his chains and groaning and hissing, he never imagined he would see his son again. Now this stranger was telling him that his daughter had a husband, she was a mother, and his Joshua was alive. Could it all be true? If it were true, why was the young man here? Why did he look so despondent? Something was dreadfully wrong. "Why haven't you mentioned news of Talia?"

Aiden finally looked helplessly, first at Luigi, who shrugged his shoulders, and then at Adil. It was Adil who finally spoke. "Talia is gone, Baba. The spirits came for the dragon but she asked for Joshua back instead. She offered her own life for his. She wanted him to have a childhood. They agreed."

Michael's shoulders slumped. His brave girl. Would happiness never be hers? Aiden spoke up quietly. "The thing is, ever since she has been gone, I have been having dreams of her. She is trapped somewhere and can't escape. I have been looking for her everywhere but I do not know the first thing about her mother's world."

Beni added solemnly, "Baba, we should go to Jaesdan. Nabia should have news for us. Before she sent me searching for you, she said she was going to call upon Caitlin's sister for help. She said you might know who I was talking about "

"Ava." Michael breathed the name aloud.

"You know her?" Beni and Adil said in unison.

"I do," said Michael.

"Let's leave at once," said Michael and Aiden together. Each recognized the fervour that burned in the eyes of the other, their mutual love for Talia, which cut across time and their separate lives, binding them together. They would do anything to get her back.

CHAPTER XXIX

Help is a luminous thing, especially if it is unexpected.
Similarly, hindsight is always twenty-twenty. Actions can be regretted at
leisure, but at a particular moment in time, we do our best with what we
know and understand.
Talia

THE MEDALLION—AVA

NABIA WAS INITIALLY STARTLED with Ava's resemblance to Caitlin, but she soon got over her surprise. As Ava formed a picture of what transpired after Caitlin disappeared, she grew increasingly dismayed. The disjointed pieces of information pouring out from the young woman told her that a great adversity had befallen Caitlin's family in Aberevon.

Caitlin was a newborn when she had hidden the truth from Siobhan, confused and frightened. But why had she, Ava, kept silent? At that time, she believed Caitlin would lose her only chance at finding real love if Siobhan knew what the prophecy was about. But could Ava now live with the consequences of her silence? In fear, Caitlin had fled from the man she loved, and now her family lay in tatters.

There was something else terrifying Ava. According to Nabia, things had started to go drastically wrong in Aberevon. Damien would be king by now. Was it a mere coincidence that tragedy had struck in Aberevon, or did the child she rescued so many years ago have something to do with all of this?

As Ava was deep in thought, she failed to see the group of men by the door. Michael and Aiden's eyes were fixed on the woman wearing a simple white tunic with flowing embroidered sleeves and a vertical slit laced at the bodice and a simple patterned cape pinned to her shoulders.

Aiden was staring at the voluminous blue curls tumbling down her shoulders. They reminded him of Talia.

Michael was transfixed because, for a moment, he believed Caitlin had returned. Then he met Nabia's gaze. She silently shook her head, a mixture of pity and understanding illuminating her expression. "Ava," said Michael. She turned towards him. He had to look away and compose himself. If it weren't for her hazel eyes, she was a dead ringer for his wife. How was he going to be able to talk to her? But for Talia's sake, he would have to get over the shock that rocked through his system every time he looked at her face.

After they told Ava what had happened, the sorceress was desolate. Things were much worse then she had imagined and it was all her fault. Caitlin and Joshua tortured. The boy killed. Caitlin taken. Talia gone.

"I should have never brought Damien here," she said, her tone conveying the deep remorse she felt.

"How could you have known?" Michael consoled her, for he

knew how much Caitlin had loved Ava. He felt a comfortable vibe of familiarity in her presence. "You were only trying to save a child. Caitlin and I were also at fault. We knew there was a prophecy hanging over our heads yet we stayed together instead of walking away. Caitlin and I knew that the consequences of us coming together might not be good; still we couldn't stay away from each other. Talia is facing the consequences of our selfishness. One could say that our love is the cause of all these problems. So, similarly, are you responsible for your action that was in complete good faith?" he asked her. "We don't want to blame anyone. We only want Talia back. Can you help us? I will do anything to get her back. The Wraith took my wife. They have to return my daughter. They can't have her too."

Michael had absolved her of her actions, but Ava was still devastated and guilt-ridden. Her silence had cost a family their lives and their togetherness. She knew it was time to talk to Siobhan.

She told the others she would return to Jaesden soon.

SIOBHAN'S REACTION WAS UNEXPECTED. She took the news of Ava's dishonesty with a quiet calm. There was neither a display of rage nor hurt.

"Why are you not upset? You don't even seem surprised," said Ava, not able to reconcile herself with Siobhan's muted response. "Taking Damien to Aberevon was my decision, so everything he did to them, the kidnapping, the imprisonment, the torture and their deaths—"

"You talk of events that have already happened, matters that cannot be changed. Did you save Damien because you knew of the wickedness he was capable of, or because he was an innocent child?" Siobhan said.

"The latter, of course," said a shocked Ava. "He was just a little boy. I never imagined he would ever be capable of so much hate. I am sorry I hid the truth from you."

"I know you would never conceal anything unless you had a good reason. I know of no one wiser than you," said Siobhan. "Being a queen does not mean just getting my way all the time or chastising those who have gone wrong. It also involves faith and belief. Besides, you have always been an embodiment of benevolence and magnanimity." Taking Ava's hand in her own, Siobhan said, "If I don't trust you, whom do I trust? In the end, it all boils down to this: did I have faith in your judgement or not? You were right. If I had known about the prophecy, I would have had to act upon the information. Didn't Caitlin deserve one chance at happiness? She couldn't have known the consequences of her actions."

"I deserve to be punished and to be banished to the great beyond like Caitlin," said Ava, her voice radiating her deep regret.

"Who will help Michael get his daughter back?" asked Siobhan. "You have a father and a husband desperately looking for someone they love, do you not? Do you want to help them?"

"More than anything in this world."

"Then let me show you how," Siobhan continued. "First, stop blaming yourself, for we can either look to place blame, or we can try to get Talia back," said Siobhan firmly. Then, in a softer voice, she added, "I think you need to forgive yourself and focus on the present. There is something that can be tried, but neither you nor I can enter the Ether World where Talia is."

"Why not?" asked a distraught Ava.

"We are connected to the Wraith, as they are our ancestors. That is the reason they prophesied Caitlin's downfall. They had a connection with her as they do with all of us. If they sense your presence, it will be too late and Talia will not be able to escape." Seeing Ava still adamant about going herself, Siobhan added, "Are you willing to risk Talia's one chance at freedom and being reunited with her family only so that you can feel good about yourself?"

"Of course not," said Ava vehemently. "But if not me, then who? Who will be willing to take such a chance? To face the Wraith?"

"Talia cannot escape alone. Someone needs to lead her out of there; and it can only be a human. In the unknown, a human can enter undetected. They never do because they do not know the way. This time, Talia's champions will have you to guide them. The spirits will not perceive them immediately. That small gap may be enough for Talia to make her escape."

"Sounds like it may work," said Ava.

"Wait. Don't be so quick to celebrate. This endeavour is very risky and there is a great chance of failure. The catch lies in form of the many traps in the unknown to prevent those who have gone into it from trying to leave. I do not know much about that place but it would suffice to say that if a person got lost in the Ether World, they may not find their way back," warned Siobhan.

CHAPTER XXX

I had given up hope, but I misjudged Aiden's love, straight and focussed as an arrow, and my father's persistence, underlying and the kind to find me even in another world.
Talia

OGETHER AGAIN

"I'VE SPOKEN TO SIOBHAN, our queen," said Ava to the attentive bunch of Talia's well-wishers after returning to Jaesdan. "Talia is in the Ether World with other sorceresses but she does not belong there. Except for Caitlin, the others went there of their own free will and have moved on," she said. Looking at Aiden, Ava continued. "Her love for you binds her so strongly to this life that she is unable to move on. She is stuck between this world and the next. Her longing for you intensifies her suffering. If she would let go, her suffering would end."

"No," said Michael and Aiden in unison.

"We have to get her back," said Aiden.

"Are you sure?" Ava asked. "This has never been done before. We are not sure it will even work. This whole gambit is fraught with risks."

"I have to take a chance. I have nothing to lose. Talia is the only reason I have been holding on for so long," said Michael.

"I am her husband. Shouldn't it be me who goes for her?" asked Aiden.

"And what of Katie and Joshua? Don't you think they deserve the love of two people who would do anything for them?" said Michael. "Being brave and being foolhardy are two different things, as Talia's mother always told her. I don't doubt your love for my daughter, but it has more value if you are here for her when she returns," said Michael. "I am her father; I am going and nobody can make me change my mind."

"I don't want to change your mind," added Luigi, "but I need to go with you." Before Michael could protest, he added, "I have nothing left here." Seeing Michael was about to insist that he stay back, Luigi silenced him. "I made a promise to my brother to try to unite your family and to protect all of you. I haven't done a great job so far."

"You have already done so much for our family," said Michael.

"Yes, I have," said Luigi bitterly, deliberately misunderstanding Michael's words of praise. "I lead Garcia to your wife and son. I watched him bind them and shove them around. I stayed quiet while they were imprisoned and tortured. I lied to my brother and used him to get information on your daughter. I lead King Damien to Talia and you. Yes, you are right, I have done enough. Yet you found it in your heart to forgive me and treat me like a brother. Let me go with you to get our girl. We have been in this to protect her from the beginning. Let me accompany you and finally find absolution. I am begging you as a friend and brother," said Luigi.

Once it was decided that Michael and Luigi would travel to the Ether World, Michael took his Jaesdan friends aside. "I must say my goodbyes now in case I don't make it back."

"Don't say that, Baba," pleaded Beni.

"You will find Talia and then return to us. No harm will befall you," Adil tried to reassure Michael.

"That is not his plan," said Nabia suddenly, comprehension dawning on her face.

"What do you mean?" asked Adil, bewilderment creeping in to his voice. "Are you calling Michael a liar?"

"Baba thinks we don't need him anymore. He also believes that when Talia returns, having Aiden, Joshua and Katie in her life will be more than enough for her. He is going to save Talia. But..." Nabia trailed off.

"But, after that?" asked a curious Luigi. He was beginning to see what Nabia was trying to tell them. He hoped the girl would confirm the truth that he was beginning to suspect too.

"Baba is also going to look for Caitlin. Since she can never return, he plans to stay back too," said Nabia her voice sorrowful.

Everyone exclaimed in shock and turned to look at Michael. He met their gaze unerringly. There was no deceit in his eyes. He wasn't about to do anything wrong, so he didn't turn away but met the questions in their eyes head on. Nabia's incredible ability to get to the heart of the matter amazed him. Now all he had to do was see if his plan would work. Luigi was more than capable of getting Talia back safely.

"Look after them," were Michael's last words to Aiden.

Ava was the only one who hung back. She knew she had no right to question Michael. All she could do was help reunite him with his lost love. It was time to play her part. She started reciting the incantation to force a gateway for the two men, an opening in the invisible shield, the Veil, between the world of magic and the world of men. On one side was Earth and on the other lay Htrae. The Ether World, or the great unknown, which held Caitlin and

Talia in its clutches, lay in between. When the gateway appeared, it sparkled and pulsated. The light beyond it was so bright that none of them could really see what lay beyond.

Michael and Luigi took one last look at the world they were leaving behind and stepped into the opening. It closed behind them. Hachim shuddered in fear. "Don't worry," Ava reassured him. "It remains accessible on the other side."

Aiden and the others could not see a thing. Nabia kept glancing at Ava as though the expression on her face would tell her what would transpire on the other side. But Ava's face was blank. Focus required her to shut down her emotions.

Would Talia be found? Would they be able to escape the clutches of the Wraith? If they were caught, would Michael and Luigi also be lost forever? Everyone had the same questions and concerns.

In the little group, everyone dealt with worry in different ways. Some had blurry eyes with unshed tears; others stared intently at the spot where the gateway had been, willing it to re-open soon. Aiden paced relentlessly for hours, stopping every few minutes to stare alternately at the Veil and then Ava, who was stoically ignoring him.

Suddenly there were loud exclamations as the gateway reappeared. Luigi stepped through pulling someone else along, a special someone who hurled herself at Aiden, hugging him so tightly he couldn't breathe. He returned the hug, holding on as tightly as he could. Talia was sobbing into his shoulder. She didn't seem happy to have escaped. She looked devastated.

Aiden embraced his wife, his relief at her return palpable. He looked at Luigi standing behind her for answers. *Where is Michael?*

"What happened in there?" asked Adil of Luigi.

"They caught up with us just as we were about to escape. Caitlin appeared out of nowhere and opened up a hidden route for us," said Luigi to his enthralled audience. "But she had to stay back to answer to the Wraith and to prevent them from stopping us."

"But as soon as Michael saw Caitlin, he left Talia's hand and went to her," added Ava. "We shouldn't be surprised. Michael never denied his plan. He loved Caitlin more than anything in this world, and she him. He saw a chance to be together and he took it. Michael knows Talia and Aiden will always love Joshua like their own child. Joshua will not be alone. He has a family to love him and care for him, but this was Michael's last chance to be reunited with Caitlin."

"You didn't stop your father, Talia?" Aiden asked in dismay.

"I could have but it wouldn't have been right. My father will never get over the loss of my mother. He has always believed that his place was by her side. When she left, he was desolate. I was the only reason he forced himself to go on. Now that I am safe and sound and have a family of my own, he knows it's okay for him to be reunited with my mother."

EPILOGUE

*J*oshua and Katie were playing together in the gardens of Syrolt. For Joshua, Katie was his best friend and sister. All things considered, Joshua seemed to be settling in very well. He had mercifully returned as a boy, minus the memories of the past. From the days gone by, he only remembered Talia as someone he loved very much. His life as the dragon, the torture he had been through, all of it had been wiped clean. Reunited with Talia, Joshua had been given a chance to live his lost life again.

Nothing could have made Michael and Caitlin happier. Their family's little knight had been given a second chance. They exchanged smiles as they watched the children from the other side of the Veil.

Soon it would be time to go, to leave their life on Earth behind and move on. As they took one last longing look at the little ones, they saw Joshua spinning around and a giggling Katie rushing in to hug him. Perfect. Could they ask for more?

Talia was no longer on the run being chased by a mad king. She had Aiden, a friend and a husband who loved her for her heart, not her powers, just as Caitlin had wished for her all those years ago.

In all her choices, Talia had always put her family before herself, no sacrifice too great. Circumstances and fate had conspired against Talia. King Damien thought he'd broken her; maybe he had, but through it all, she was never lost. Her faith, hope and thirst for vengeance had burned bright, showing her the way from darkness into the light. The fury of the tempestuous storm chasing her had faded into nothing with Damien's death and Joshua's return. She was finally free.

Before she had stepped free of the Ether World with Luigi, she had a short, bittersweet reunion with her mother and father while Luigi kept an eye out for the Wraith. In that one moment, they had all embraced, needing no words. However much she wanted them to return with her, she knew they couldn't. Caitlin couldn't step out of her prison and Michael didn't want to part from her again. It didn't matter in the end because Talia knew they would always remain in her heart. They would always be a part of her and Joshua. She couldn't bring herself to force her father to return with her. His place had always been with her mother. Without Caitlin, he was bereft and rudderless. He was like one half of a soul. It was time for all of them to be complete and broken no more.

Michael and Caitlin were finally together, this time for eternity. Caitlin had nothing to fear anymore, no shadows or ghosts from the past chasing her. She was finally at peace. Their life had meandered through a rocky road of both good times and bad. And now in a different time and place, they were together again, their love constant and just the same.

Their hands intertwined, Michael and Caitlin took the first step deep into the unknown without the fear of a dark past catching up with them, the agony of being prised away from each other or the pain of regret. The passage of time felt immaterial, almost as if life had gone full circle and brought them right back to where they had started—a new beginning.

The Wraith no longer wished to separate them. They had prophesised this love after all. If Caitlin, the first of her kind, the first guardian from the Well of Creation, was willing to give it all up for love, who were they to stop her? Love, it seemed, was even more powerful than any prophecy, for only love has the power to mend that which is broken.

The End...

AFTERWORD

Dear Reader, I hope you enjoyed reading about Talia and Caitlin. The women in *Broken* are strong women who face difficult, if not impossible, circumstances. They make choices you may not agree with, but do what they think is right at that time. Please don't judge them too harshly. Theirs is a fantasy world, but in the real world too, the one we live in, we make difficult decisions every day and sometimes find it is possible to be *Broken* but not lost. Michael and Aiden are protective but not overbearing. Similarly, in our lives, guys, real men with hearts, not necessarily muscles, often enrich our lives.

Please let me know your views and feelings on this book by leaving a review for *Broken* on Amazon or Goodreads. Just a few thoughts (minus spoilers) would be much appreciated.

Thank you so much for reading.
With kind regards,
Ivy Logan

ACKNOWLEDGMENTS

A big thank you to my dearest mum, Ivy, my dad, Francis, and my sister, Karen, for inspiring me to see the wonder in life a long time ago and for supporting me even today. My journey began with you.

I couldn't have done this without my husband, Ian, who set me down this path and has supported me in every way possible. You have allowed me to remain in my dream world and thus create *Broken*. You are my rock.

Thank you to my children, who have remained supportive and encouraging even though I ignored you both in favour of Talia.

Vishvesh Desai and your team at Ideascope, you have been a friend and a guiding light, always there for me. Could I have done this without you? I don't think so.

Abbie, my editor, it felt great knowing you were there to answer any query, to clarify any doubt. I depend on you.

Ann Walker, you were the beta reader Talia needed to emerge into the light. Your consistent and encouraging feedback was my greatest friend.

My dear friend, author Verity Short, thank you. Your beta inputs made a great difference to the book.

A big mention to all my friends, including those on Facebook, Twitter and in the blog world, for always supporting me and answering my many questions.

And thank you Mario for making Talia real for the readers of *Broken* and for me.

Coming Soon...

METAMORPHOSIS
What if your entire life was a lie?
The Breach Chronicles Book II

The luminescence and incandescent beauty of the rare pink diamonds of Peradora cannot disguise the unhappy life of Amelia, who has always believed she is a harbinger of death and bad luck, for she killed her parents when she was just five.

Amelia is desperately attracted to a handsome orphan, Marc, who is always rescuing her from near fatal accidents. However, Marc views her as a magnet for danger and is anxious to avoid her.

Her eighteenth birthday brings a revelation—her entire life has been a lie. She is given the gift of shape—shifting—by the queen of the sorceresses, but this gift could take her down a path from which there is no return.

Meanwhile, danger from the realm of supernaturals shadows Peradora. The only person standing in its way is Amelia.

Share Amelia's journey of self-discovery. Watch her blossom and come into her own as she looks for the hero within. Does her metamorphosis become the clarion call of a revolution, or is it the reason for her desolation?

Do write to me at ivylogan9@gmail.com if you would like to be a part of the exclusive group giving feedback on the final touches of Amelia's story, or if you would like contests or snippets of the story.

ABOUT THE AUTHOR

Ivy Logan is extremely passionate about stories, especially those steeped in mythical folklore and ancient myths and legends suffused with the magic of unique realms and supernatural worlds.

Through her stories, Ivy Logan invites her readers to a world of magic and wonder, urging them to discover themselves through this ongoing journey.

If you think you have an experience worth sharing that exemplifies the tag line 'Broken But Not Lost', or a special relationship like Caitlin and Michael or Talia and Aiden, do write to me. It would be wonderful to hear from you.

www.ivylogan.wordpress.com
ivylogan9@gmail.com
www.facebook.com/ivyloganauthor
www.twitter.com/ivyloganauthor

Printed in Great Britain
by Amazon

79820322R00129